Cthul'
to claim the Ea
The G
upon Hum
Cthulhi
to prepare
**Thus, Cthulhu now answers humanity's questions
to help them better themselves.**

Dear Cthulhu,

It turns out they've been having a bullying problem at my child's school. I've been getting notes from the principal about it for weeks. Then I was called in for a conference with his teacher and the principal. Imagine my shock and dismay when I learned that the bully was none other than my own son. I mean, I knew he had issues after his mother ran off and left us to join the professional bodybuilder and cooking circuit. I miss her too; especially the times and she'd bench press me during sex while she made a chocolate soufflé.

And it didn't help matters when Junior got into the stash of anabolic steroids his mother left behind. Junior began to look like a 4-foot version of the Incredible Hulk, minus the green skin. I had pretended to ignore it because Junior misses his mommy and his taking her pills made him feel closer to her.

Turns out he's been having anger issues and beating up the other kids at school. I sat him down so we could have a father-son chat and I explained that bullying and beating up weaker people was wrong. He responded by wrestling me to the ground, stealing my wallet, and giving me a wedgie.

I later learned he would've been suspended earlier except he had beaten up his teacher and she was afraid of him too.

I don't seem to be getting through to Junior and he seems so angry all the time. I'm worried if this keeps up that he won't make it into the third grade. What can I do?

– Pounded Poppa in Poughkeepsie

Dear Pounded,

Anabolic steroids are not intended for a human whom Cthulhu surmises must be about eight years of age. Even on adult humans, they have been shown to have various negative side effects, not the least of which is something called roid rage. The first thing you should do find all the steroids and destroy them. Next, take your son to a competent physician and get him a full checkup. Perhaps even have him talk to a guidance counselor at the school about issues dealing with his mother's abandonment of her family. Do all this and in a few months, the situation should be more under control as his body returns to normal.

In the meantime, take a page from your wife's book and start working out. There is no way a man, even a tiny one, should be beaten up by an eight-year-old.

That or – as long as you do not mind the devastating long term effects of steroids on a child – consider pitching a show about child professional wrestlers – call it CPW. It will give your offspring a place to work off his roid rage and earn some money for college.

DEAR CTHULHU™ Series
HAVE A DARK DAY - GOOD ADVICE FOR BAD PEOPLE
CTHULHU KNOWS BEST - WHAT WOULD CTHULHU DO?
CTHULHU HAPPENS - CTHULHU EXPLAINS IT ALL

THE MURPHY'S LORE™ SERIES
TALES FROM BULFINCHE'S PUB
FOOLS' DAY: *A Tale From Bulfinche's Pub*
THROUGH THE DRINKING GLASS: *Tales From Bulfinche's Pub*
SHADOW OF THE WOLF: *A Tale From Bulfinche's Pub*
REDEMPTION ROAD
BARTENDER OF THE GODS: *Tales From Bulfinche's Pub*

THE MURPHY'S LORE AFTER HOURS™ UNIVERSE
NIGHTCAPS - *AFTER HOURS Vol. 1*
EMPTY GRAVES - *AFTER HOURS Vol. 2*
THE MUG LIFE - *AFTER HOURS Vol. 3*
FAIRY WITH A GUN: *The Collected Terrorbelle*™
FAIRY RIDES THE LIGHTNING: *a Terrorbelle*™ *novel*
TERRORBELLE THE UNCONQUERED
EAD TO RITES: *The DMA Casefiles of Agent Karver*™
RITES OF PASSAGE *(with John French)*
LORE & DYSORDER: *The Hell's Detective*™ *Mysteries*
BY DARKNESS CURSED: *a Hexcraft collection*
BY INVOCATION ONLY: *a Hexcraft novel*

MURPHY'S LORE STARTENDERS™
STARTENDERS - CONSTELLATION PRIZE

MYSTIC INVESTIGATORS SERIES
MYSTIC INVESTIGATORS - MEAN STREETS - FEAR TO TREAD *(COMING SOON)*
OMNIBUS EDITIONS
SHADOWS & BRIMSTON *(includes BULLETS & BRIMSTONE and FROM THE SHADOWS)*
with John French
ONCE UPON IN CRIME *(includes ONCE MORE UPON A TIME and PARTNERS IN CRIME)*
with Diane Raetz

The Playworlds
AS THE GEARS TURN: *Tales From Steamworld*

Xiles
EXILE & ENTRANCE

OTHER BOOKS
NEW BLOOD edited by Diane Raetz & Patrick Thomas
CAMELOT 13 edited by John L. French & Patrick Thomas

THE JACK GARDNER MYSTERIES
THE ASSASSINS' BALL

Cthulhu Happens

The Collected Advice Columns of

Vol. 5

Patrick Thomas

PADWOLF PUBLISHING INC.
WWW.PADWOLF.COM
www.facebook.com/Padwolf

WWW.PATTHOMAS.NET
WWW.DEARCTHULHU.COM

www.facebook.com/PatrickThomasAuthor

I_PatrickThomas @ Twitter

CTHULHU HAPPENS
The Collected Advice Columns of Dear Cthulhu Vol. 5

© 2018 Patrick Thomas

Portions of this book have appeared in column form in the following magazines: Tales From The Talisman, Nth Degree, and The Realm Beyond.

Book edited by John L. French

Cover Art by Patrick Thomas

Dear Cthulhu is © & TM Patrick Thomas

All rights reserved. No part of this book may be reproduced or transmitted in any means electronic or mechanical, including recording, photocopying or by any information storage and retrieval system, without the written permission of the copyright holder. And do you really want to mess with Cthulhu?

This is a work of fiction and satire. No similarity between any of the names, characters, persons, situations and/or institutions and those of any preexisting person or institution is intended and any similarity which may exist is purely coincidental.

ISBN 10 digit 1-890096-76-8 and 13 digit 978-1-890096-76-2
First printing. Printed in the USA

If you have any additional questions that Cthulhu can answer, and Cthulhu can answer all questions, Dear Cthulhu welcomes letters and questions at DearCthulhu@dearcthulhu.com. All letters become the property of Dear Cthulhu and may be used in future columns. Sending financial offerings along with your questions is not necessary but is always appreciated.

Anyone foolish enough to follow Dear Cthulhu's advice does so at their own peril.

*For those whose advice
makes the world a better place*

Cthulhu Happens

Dear Cthulhu,

I am a bibliophile and I couldn't be more embarrassed by my condition. I was raised in a very religious household and that's where my attraction to the Bible started. Yes, I'm a man who is sexually aroused by the Good Book.

I think I can trace it all back to my early teens when I first started noticing girls. Like any hormonal teenage boy, I had needs. But such topics were not discussed in my house. I had my own tablet to surf the Internet and our neighbors' property had a pond where beavers had built a dam. I thought it was interesting so I did an Internet search on beavers. The results I got back had very little to do with the animal but were very arousing to my teenage mind and I did what came naturally and touched myself in a sinful manner.

It was my first time so I didn't think enough to lock my bedroom door and my mother walked in carrying laundry, saw what I was doing, and freaked out. She dropped the laundry on the floor, picked up the Bible off my nightstand, and bent me over the bed and started spanking me with it. My bottom was bare as I'd already removed my pants to make the sinful touching easier. As my mother spanked me, I could still see and hear the video of a woman screaming things I'd never heard before and for the first time in my life, I climaxed.

My mother made me go to religious counseling to try and undo the damage the secular word had done. She took away my tablet and the Internet. She even threw out our clothes catalogs because they had pictures of women in underwear. She got rid of everything that might be stimulating to a young boy approaching manhood, but she left the Bible. Seeing the Good Book there made me remember the scene in the video which made me excited. I ended up carving out a section in the middle of the Bible and used it for purposes that no good religious person ever should.

Since I wasn't using my hand or having premarital sex with a

The Collected Columns Volume 5 • 7

woman, my teenage mind assumed it was okay. My mind played back those scenes from the videos.

Fast forward 10 years. I've had a few relationships

I've moved away from my parents' church and religious teachings. I've had relationships with women, some of them even sexual, but I always have trouble finishing. It's gotten to the point where I have to have the Bible somewhere in the room so I can focus on it in order to climax.

I know there's something wrong with me, but I can't figure out how to fix it. Is there a support group for people with my kink, one that might have some suggestions for how to stop it?

– Bible Thumper in Biloxi

Dear Biloxi,

First off, learn to use a dictionary. The term bibliophile does not mean what you think it does. It is used to describe someone who enjoys books and reading, not someone who wishes to procreate with the Bible, although I suppose it is better than trying to do so with the Necronomicon. Your manhood would be burned away if you tried that.

It sounds as if your first sexual experience was interrupted and unfortunately, the spanking with the religious text simply imprinted itself on you, supplanting normal arousing markers like human women with something else. There are those would tell you to seek counseling, but Cthulhu is not one of those ilk.

You need to take control of your life and your mind. Try to re-create your initial experience, going so far as to find a similar video if not the same one. Recreate the conditions and have an attractive woman walking with laundry in her arms. If you are not a relationship with anyone who would be willing, there are prostitutes who would do this for money and it would likely not be the oddest request they've ever had. Have her yell at you about how horrible what you did was and then take your Bible and throw it away. Have her smack you with her hand and then proceed to finish the act of procreation with you. Try some variance on it, getting rid of the object of your lust and replacing it with more conventional urges and hopefully this will fade for you. This doesn't work, try to find an understanding partner who is willing to perhaps wear the book around her body as lingerie, which will allow you to perform more normally.

Dear Cthulhu,

I'm a grown man, but I still sleep with a teddy bear. I know that sounds a bit sad and maybe a little creepy, but my bear has been my best friend for most of my life. I never really had much of a chance to have *people* friends when I was younger. My family was poor and mean. My father beat me and my mother, at least until the day he hit her too hard and she died. I remember it well because it was the week before Christmas when I was seven years old. A charity made sure I got a gift and it was Teddy.

I cried myself to sleep every night for six months, worrying that my dad was coming back. Fortunately, he was convicted and after that day, I've never seen him again. I was moved from foster home to foster home, never quite fitting in. I guess I was a little broken inside. Not that people didn't try to help, but then I became more of an oddity than a person. The kids at a new school would find out what my father had done and they treated me like I was some tabloid news story, asking about details about the beatings we got and how he killed her, what her dead body looked like, and other insensitive nonsense.

Sadly, that was the story of my life, but the one constant is every night I went to sleep holding Teddy. No matter how bad the day was, that bear helped me get through it.

Fast-forward – I'm twenty-two years old with a decent job and I actually have a girlfriend. "Amy" is wonderful.

I didn't think it was possible for me to bond so closely with another person, but Amy proved me wrong. We live in the same building and we started out smiling as we passed each other. Then she said hi, I said hi back and before you know it, we got to talking. Real conversations. Then she actually asked *me* out for dinner. Things were going great. Then on our second date, she asked me why I never talked about my family. I guess I was quiet for a long time, but then I risked it all and told her everything.

I was terrified that it would change everything, that I'd become the living freak show again, but instead of looking at me judgmentally Amy opened up her arms and pulled me in for a hug. She held me right there in the restaurant and didn't let go. I'm not ashamed to admit that I cried.

What started out as tears of sorrow ended up as tears of joy as I realized that there was actually someone who cared about me. It was wonderful.

Our relationship progressed physically until I finally spent the night at her place. The problem was afterward I couldn't sleep. Not without Teddy. By morning I knew two things. One, I was in love. And two, I was unable to sleep without Teddy. After a week I was barely able to function at my job and was worried about getting fired. I came up with a plan. I would wait until she fell asleep and then sneak back to my apartment and get some shut eye. This worked out okay for about a month because I set my alarm for half an hour before she got up. I'd run out to the coffee shop and bring back a bag breakfast for us both.

It all fell apart this morning when I showed up egg sandwiches and coffees. Amy was awake and had been for a couple of hours. It seems she had gotten up to go the bathroom and realized I wasn't there. We got into a fight and she accused me of sneaking out on her see somebody else.

Apparently, an old boyfriend had done her wrong and it was a touchy subject. I told her I would never, ever cheat on her. She was the only good thing that ever happened to me in my life and that I would never do anything that could to hurt her, but I stopped short of telling her about Teddy.

I was worried about how she was going to react. Kids in the foster homes – and even a few of the foster parents – had laughed and mocked me for sleeping with Teddy. I was afraid Amy would think I was a child or worse, laugh at me. I don't know where I'd find the strength to go on if that happened.

I have no friends or family to ask which is why I am writing you. What should I do?

– Guy with a Teddy in Tallahassee

Dear Tallahassee,

Humanity manages to shock even great Cthulhu on occasion. Not by the acts of depravity and evil which they inflict on each other, but instead by their lack of being able to predict what their fellow humans will do. For instance, say a person constantly abuses another person, treats them like trash, and takes advantage of them at every turn. Why would that person assume the abuser was ever going to do something different? The ideas that a stranger or prince from Nigeria is going to give someone money for no reason is ludicrous, yet people fall for these scams every day.

By the same reasoning, you are assuming that this woman who has proven herself to you to be a kind and compassionate person, someone who took you at face value with all your flaws and showed you kindness and compassion is suddenly going to turn into a monster because you tell her about a childhood trauma. You sleep with a stuffed animal because it has comforted you. Cthulhu gets letters every day about people who have problems with their partners and this does not even register as a blip on my problem scale. I suspect that this Amy will understand if you tell her what is going on. She may even be willing to let your stuffed bear share the same bed with the two of you so you can sleep and what's more, sleep with her.

Provided you have not left out any important details, like the fact that you are also procreating with this bear, Cthulhu suggests you tell her everything and would bet that you find yourself pleasantly surprised at the results.

Cthulhu Happens

Dear Cthulhu,

The uproar in this country over creepy clowns is ruining my life. I am a professional clown and make my living doing children's birthday parties. I am a high-quality clown and it takes me 45 minutes to an hour to do my makeup, which means I go to my gigs dressed as a clown. Because I'm a clown, I can't afford a car, which means I take the bus to get where I'm going.

For years, it's been a fun experience. I wave to people and make balloon animals for children and anybody else who wants them. I like to think that I made public transportation fun for the other riders.

Lately, it's all changed. With all these reports around the country of creepy clowns just standing and staring at people, folks get freaked out really easily. I didn't realize how bad it was until I got on the bus to go to a gig last week. I made a balloon animal for a little girl and her mother pulled her away from me rather than let her accept it. The next time I was on the bus a gang of high school kids started yelling at me for staring at them – I wasn't. I was just sitting forward on the bus and they happen to be in front of me. They beat the crap out of me.

Then the thing that to cap it all off was I was hired to do a kid's birthday party in an apartment building. They wanted me to be a surprise, so they had me wait in the hall. The neighbors were so freaked out they called the cops. I tried to explain, but instead of listening one of the cops tazed me. I woke up in a holding cell.

I can't take it anymore. What can I do to convince people that clowns aren't a menace, but funny and friendly people?

– Clown with a Red Nose and steam coming out of his ears in San Francisco.

Dear Red Nose,

The clown thing is been building for years with people who have a clown phobia. Add in political correctness where scaring someone is wrong so it has only a matter of time before people came after the clowns. This current trend has been rumored by some to have started as a publicity stunt for a movie, but the movie producers have denied it.

Changing public perception on a large scale requires control of the news media. The news and other media, or a very strong social media presence and several things that go viral. You could try to do a happy video about clowns doing good deeds or helping people walk across the street, but the odds of something like that going viral are not very good.

Your best bet is to not look like a clown in public until this current perception changes. You can make it part of your requirements to be hired that you have to be allowed a room to put on your makeup at the site and then take it off again before you leave. If that is not practical, then at least don't look like a clown. Wearing normal appearing clothing will probably be helpful such as jeans and a loose fitting hoodie that can drape your face in shadow. Keep the red nose off and wear a pair of dark sunglasses. Pick up a newspaper and put it in front of your face so the people around you don't realize you have clown makeup on.

And if confronted again, deny being a clown and tell them you are a mime, which would be kind of ruining the point of that profession, but most people would not grasp that. Throw off any attackers by pretending to be in an invisible box and then fake suffocation or beating yourself up.

Cthulhu Happens

Dear Cthulhu,

I'm not so recently single. Men don't seem to care much for me. I'm not attractive in the traditional way or any of the non-traditional ways either.

My roommate is a whore. Well, I guess technically she's a slut because she gives it away instead of taking money. She was making fun of my inability to get a man when she can get two or three on a good day.

She bet me that she could dress one of the birds at the ostrich farm she works in a dress and a wig and put it on the Trinder hook up app and she would get more swipes than me.

I know I'm not the best-looking woman in the world, but it seemed ridiculous to me so I bet her a hundred bucks she was wrong.

Turns out I got three good swipes and Ozzette the Ostrich got fifty. It turns out there is a kink fetish out there where men are physically attracted to giant birds.

Roomie decided to set up a dating service for these perverts.

I told her I thought was she was doing was disgusting and immoral.

Even though my roomie will have sex for free, she decided to have these men pay her to have sex with the bird. I told her that was even worse. Then she told me gets two grand a pop and makes the guys pay for the hotel room. She uses the trailer from work to sneak Ozzette out and back. Roomie charges extra if they want the wig and dress on Ozzette. She gives the bird one of her valiums so it's relaxed for its date.

I was about to tell her she had to move out and I was calling the cops when she offered to make me an equal partner. Turns out there are a lot of these horny bird humpers and she needs help to get another bird out so she can service two of the sickos at once.

I'm torn. I think it's wrong and is hurting the animals, but I make only a buck over minimum wage and if I do this for a

year, I could buy a house for cash. However, I am a little mad at Ozzette for getting more guys than me. And more sex. I'm so horny I could cry.
What should I do?
-Uglier Than an Ostrich in a Dress in Utah

Dear Uglier,
It is indeed immoral and wrong to prostitute these animals but immoral and wrong are two things than humans are exceptionally good at. Although Cthulhu would enjoy watching you trying to do this to a byakhee or shantak.
You need to determine what kind of person you are and want to be. A good person would not do this regardless of financial gain. A bad person would figure a way to not only profit but not get caught and even expand the business like your roommate.
Decide which kind of person you are and choose accordingly.
Another option is you could dress up in an ostrich suit and offer your procreational services as an alternate option to these men, perhaps at a discounted price. You may find some takers, make some cash and be able to procreate, all while protecting the animal.

Cthulhu Happens

Dear Cthulhu,

I am recently single after a contentious and messy divorce. My ex-wife messed up my head and my spirit and I was very anxious to get back and swim around the dating pool a bit. I wasn't looking for anything serious, at least not at first. After the terrible time in my life that my marriage was, I just wanted to have some fun.

I tried bunch of dating apps, but no one swiped me. I tried those dating sites that had applications, but I didn't match up with anybody.

Finally, I signed up for an app called Prêt à tout, which I didn't find out until much later was French for desperate and game for anything. Suddenly I was Mr. Popular. The first day, my inbox had 10 messages from people who wanted to date me. Although to be honest, I'm pretty sure three of them were men dressing as women, and another profile picture look like someone had put a dress and a wig on an ostrich.

There was one woman whose profile picture was absolutely gorgeous. We communicated by messaging and text for a while. She seemed a little bit too perfect so I was a little bit concerned that she might be someone trying to catfish me. That's when you meet somebody online who's pretending to be someone they're not.

I suggested we video chat and was thrilled when she agreed. If anything, she was more beautiful than her picture and she was sweet and nice, nothing like my mean and vicious ex. It wasn't very long before I liked her a lot and we agreed to meet for coffee. She even hinted that if I played my cards right, I might get lucky.

It all fell apart soon after I arrived at the coffee shop. I arrived first, which was for her probably a good thing. If I've been the second one there, I probably would've run off and never looked back.

Susie showed up wearing a wedding dress and veil, with her Chihuahua on a leash dressed in a tuxedo. It wasn't Halloween.

She sat down, leaned over and kissed me on the lips and told me she was so happy I came. I asked her what the deal with the outfit was, if maybe she was going to a costume party.

She laughed as if I'd said the funniest thing and told me I was being silly. She told me that this was our wedding. She didn't want to waste a lot of time getting to know each other and going through the motions because she knew in her heart that we were soul mates destined to be together forever and ever.

I told her I'd come for coffee, not a lifelong commitment. She leaned over and whispered in my ear that getting lucky tonight was a sure thing on a honeymoon.

Then she got down on one knee, pulled out a ring box and asked me to marry her. I was stunned and didn't say anything. Instead, I looked up and noticed suddenly that we were surrounded by people dressed in suits and gowns. Susie had invited her friends and family. Not to mention my friends and family! She had my parents flown in. There was even a justice of the peace. My best friend from high school was standing there in a tux ready to be my best man. It was insane.

Instead of answering, I asked her how she got a hold of all my family and friends. Turns out she got in contact with my ex-wife who gave her all the information. My ex makes a lot more money than I do and in the settlement ended up having to pay me alimony. I guess in her twisted mind, this would help her get out of paying.

I told Susie that it was crazy. We just met and I couldn't marry her. I probably said it a little louder than I should have, because Susie ran off crying.

My own mother came over to me and smacked me in the back of the head and told me that I wasn't being the type of person she raised me to be. You see, Susie was obviously pregnant. It seems she and my ex-wife conspired to tell everybody that I was the father. My ex even told my mother that Susie was the reason we broke up because I'd been cheating on her. Nothing could be further than the truth. I was faithful, but my wife cheated on me with a heavy metal barbershop quartet for over a year before I found out. What made it worse is she asked me to buy her their CD – *Headbanger Adeline* – for her for her birthday and I did.

My father told me I need to do the right thing so my child wasn't illegitimate. I tried explaining to everyone that this was the first time I'd ever met Susie in person. In all our video chats, I'd only seen her from the chest up so I had no idea she was pregnant. I told everyone that that there is no way the child could be mine.

Susie may have been crazy, but she is well-liked in town. I have become a pariah for leaving her at the instant altar. No one seems to care that the wedding was the first time we met. My own parents have cut off contact with me and told me I'm out of their will. Not that that's a big deal because they don't have anything, but it's still frustrating that they believe a stranger over me.

Susie even took me to court for child support, but I insisted on a DNA test which proved I wasn't the father. The only one the results mattered to is the judge. No one else seems to care that it proves me right.

What can I do to get people to stop hating me?
– Single and Resisting a Hostile Takeover

Dear Hostile,

First off, you should cease being concerned about what others think of you. You have proof that the child is not yours, so you should be happy with that. The people judging you sound like busybodies who are poking their noses into your life because they're unhappy with their own. The fact that your own progenitors would take the side of a stranger over yours does not speak highly of them, although it does speak volumes about your relationship. You mentioned that your parents had been flown in for the surprise ceremony. This tells me that you have managed to live your life so that you are far enough away from your parents that you do not have to visit them for more than major life events and holidays. Since you worked hard to get them out of your life your day-to-day life, stop being concerned by what they think.

It sounds as if you weren't happy with your first marriage, so it is unlikely you would have been happy in a second one that was thrown upon you. Not only that but if you gave in to your would-be spouse so quickly it would set the tone for the rest of your marital life. She would expect you to give into every demand she asked of you because none of them would be as extreme as the one you've already agreed to.

One thing you failed to consider entirely is that your ex bride did not just go along with Susie but cooked up this entire thing as a scam. You mentioned that you had difficulty finding dates previously, yet a beautiful woman suddenly throws herself at you, willing to spend the rest of her life with you based on a few emails and video calls. This is suspicious to Cthulhu. You haven't changed your appearance or economic status, so why would you suddenly be able to attract such a beautiful woman? Cthulhu suspects that your ex orchestrated the entire thing, hoping you would be pressured or surprised enough to give in, perhaps to appease your parents and public opinion. The moment you said I do, her need to pay alimony would end. The new bride could then divorce you the next day, but the need for alimony payments would remain null and void. If it's a large amount, perhaps she offered this pregnant woman a sum of money if she managed to snare you in matrimony. Then as the husband, your name would've been on the birth certificate and you would've been stuck with child support for the rest of your life.

Despite what everyone else has told you, it sounds as if you've made the right decision for you. Human opinion on scandals is fickle and the attention on yours will waver as soon as a new one comes along. Go about your business and ignore the busybodies.

And send her to me. I can always use another Bride of Cthulhu. They never seem to last past the honeymoon and her Chihuahua will make a tasty snack for after.

Cthulhu Happens

Dear Cthulhu,

I have a problem with my daughter. She's 11 years old and lately, she's been going to a lot of birthday parties at Murray Mozzarella's, the place that does all the kids' birthday parties and has a rat in a tuxedo sing and dance with the kids. They get a bunch of tokens to play games to get tickets that they exchange for prizes.

It seems all well and good, except my daughter has become obsessed with the place. More than that, she's addicted. She started going on her way home from school and spending all her allowance on tokens. Then she started taking money out of my wallet and my wife's purse to buy more tokens. When we found out we banned her from the place and told her she wouldn't be getting an allowance again until she paid off what she stole from us. It'll take about three and half years.

All was well and good for a week, then we noticed her coming home with toys. At first, it was a whistle or bouncing ball, then a stuffed animal. Last night she came home with a full-sized two-person kayak. We asked her where she was getting stuff from. She told us she found it in the neighbor's garbage, but we didn't believe her. After we threatened to take away her phone, she finally broke.

Turns out she'd used the scanner and printer at school to counterfeit the Murray Mozzarella tickets. She started printing off the tickets at school and trading them in for the small prizes. Then she realized she could sell them to the other kids and she made enough that she bought her own computer, scanner, and ticket paper, and set it up in our attic. She's making enough that she was able to hire her own Goober driver to take her to and from Murray Mozzarella's.

Then she handed us a stack of cash that paid off all the money she took. She still had a pile of cash in her room. We sat down and figured out it turned out she was making $1000 a week selling these tickets to the other kids. That's more than I make it my job.

At first, we grounded her and banned her from doing it. As I thought more about it, the more it that seemed like a good idea. There's no law against counterfeiting tickets far as I know, and if she kept it up she could pay off her education at a good college in less than two years. Not to mention the kayak was a birthday gift for me. It's been something I've been wanting for a long time, but just could never afford, which was very sweet of her. I could even drive my daughter around to other Murray Mozzarella's in the area to reduce the risk of her getting caught.

Part of me is even considering quitting my day job and going into the ticket counterfeiting business with my daughter full-time. My question is would I be setting a bad example for her and would that make me a bad parent?

– Father of A Counterfeiting Daughter In Cheektowaga

Dear Cheektowaga,

Your daughter should be praised, not punishment or scolded. The child saw something she wanted and figured out a way to get it and then some. There are millions of adults who don't have her intelligence, ingenuity, let alone her work ethic.

I think you should allow your daughter to continue what she's doing. Your idea of varying the places where she selling is wise. Even though it is not illegal, if the store owners figure out what you are doing, they will change the tickets and make them harder to counterfeit. You should be prepared for this eventuality and the possibility that the bottom will fall out of the counterfeit ticket market at any time. It is because of this it would be very foolish of you to quit your job for something that could go on for years or just weeks. Plus, if your daughter is caught, because she is a minor sure likely just get a slap on the wrist and be banned from the establishment. If an adult is caught they could trump up some criminal charges as well as a civil suit.

Not to mention the idea of an adult male hanging around a place frequented by young children trying to sell them things would be viewed as creepy. If you got you caught you could possibly be in a lot more trouble than just counterfeit tickets if your actions are misunderstood.

Dear Cthulhu,

I'm a 40-year-old woman and I've just found out that my mother is a cat burglar. I'm not talking the exciting kind that breaks into rich people's houses and steals their jewels. No, my mother goes around stealing actual cats.

I live a couple of hours away and can only visit occasionally. After my dad died, Mom went to a dark place for a while because she got lonely. Then she adopted Fluffy, a very nice cat from the animal shelter. She liked Fluffy so much, Mom went back to the animal shelter and adopted another. And another. At five, the animal shelter cut her off because they felt that was more cats think then were safe to live in a small house.

Mom wasn't about to be deterred. She drove to the surrounding towns and staked out people's houses. She'd look for felines she liked and then steal the cats. She developed a bunch of different methods.

She designed a box that she puts a chuck of cheese filled with catnip in. The cat smells the cheese, goes in the box and the door shuts. Mom takes the box home and bam, she has a new cat.

For those homes that let the cats use a pet door, she built a device that she sticks through the pet door from an old person grabber thing they use to pick up stuff off the floor. The thing bends up, she pulls and twists and viola, the door opens, letting her steal the cat. Plus, any toys and cat food that are lying around as well.

I hadn't been to visit in a couple months so I was shocked when I walked into her house and counted 45 cats! The entire wall of her spare bedroom is lined with litter boxes. The place smells like cat pee.

Mom said the cats make her happy and that each and every one of them is much a child to her as I am. Some were even more so because none of them went off to live her own life and leave their mother. (Mom's a bit passive aggressive.)

When I suggested to mom that she might have a problem,

she told me to mind my own business or I'd be out of the will.

Mom's not rich but the mortgage on the house is paid off, and when she eventually does check out it would be worth a nice chunk of change, assuming someone could ever get the smell of cat pee out of it.

I'm worried about my mother's health. I've always heard the term crazy cat lady and feel my mother definitely qualifies. Is that an actual real disease that I could have a shrink diagnose my mother with so she can be deemed incompetent? If so, could I be put in charge of all her finances and make sure the cats get back to their rightful owners? Plus, I'd be able to make sure my inheritance will be worth something when the time comes.

Do you have any suggestions to offer me?

– Devoted Daughter with Forty-Five Furry Siblings

Dear Devoted,

It does sound as if your mother has a problem. That number of cats is too much for any normal person without a farm or other large property to take care of.

Plus, she is breaking into other people's houses to steal cats. This could lead to her being arrested or shot or mauled by a dog who doesn't want his feline companion stolen.

While crazy cat lady is not recognized as a medical diagnosis to the best of my knowledge, it does sound as if your mother does need help.

Living with that much cat waste could make her sick. Cat feces often carry toxoplasmosis which can cause all sorts of neurological brain damage to those who are immunodeficient or if anyone pregnant should visit her. If your mother gets sick she could end up even worse off than she is now. You might want to speak to an animal control officer and then a lawyer to see if you can have the animals returned without criminal charges being brought against your mother. If not, send them Cthulhu's way and Cthulhu will whip us some Hollandaise sauce and make the evidence disappear for you.

Your mother should be able to keep at least the five she got herself, and then perhaps she could volunteer at an animal shelter to take care of animals in need which would satisfy her needs as well as help the animals.

Cthulhu Happens

Dear Cthulhu,

I recently read your response to the guy who slept with a Teddy bear and it inspired me to write as well. It's not me, but my new girlfriend. When we first started seeing each other, she told me that she slept with a doll. I didn't think much of it at the time. After a few months, we got intimate with each other, but "Annie" always seemed bored by me in bed. I'm no Don Juan but I've had a few girlfriends and never really had any complaints before. Dolly would always get up and leave when we were done, telling me she couldn't sleep without her doll. After this happened a few times, I suggested we stay at her place so she could use sleep with her doll. We go in to her bedroom and nature takes its car and we hop into bed, but there's no doll anywhere to be seen. She rubs my head when we're done. Before I know it, I'm out cold. I wake up sometime later to hear her yelling like she's a porn star. She barely even raised her voice above a whisper with me. The noises were coming from her walk-in closet. I had no idea what was going on, but I suspected she was cheating on me while I was in her apartment and I wanted to find out. When I opened the door, I got the shock of my life. Annie was cheating on me with her doll. However, this wasn't some infant from the cabbage patch or one that needs its diaper changed. It was a fully automated Japanese male sex robot. It was designed to feel and look human, at least from the waist up. From the waist down, it was a whole another manner. Its man parts were as long and wide as my forearm and had more settings and speeds than a blender. What's worse is she saw me but didn't stop. Instead, she held up one finger as if telling me to wait a minute, then she twisted both of her doll's nipples which shifted it into overdrive. The whole apartment began to shake from the thrusting and vibrating this thing was putting off. It was a personalized earthquake. The lights in the apartment even dimmed and the screams she gave off had my ears ringing for twenty minutes.

I obviously wanted to have a conversation about what had

just happened, but Dolly just curled up in the crook of this sex doll's armpit and put her head on his chest. She told me that she got the doll about a year ago and ever since then human men haven't been able to satisfy her needs. I asked if she's willing to get rid of the doll and give me an opportunity to try. She said "not a chance" then fell asleep on the robot's chest. The mechanical creep even squeezed her butt.

We talked some more in the morning and I found out where I stood. It seems her mother was bugging her to get a boyfriend, so to keep her mom off her back, she was willing to date me and give me sex whenever I wanted so long as I was willing to go with her to all family dinners and function as her boyfriend.

Now I have a decision to make. I don't think I could deal with a regular woman cheating on me with a robot, but Dolly is super-hot, like a solid nine. Most of the women I date are fives and sixes and most of them weren't willing to give me sex anytime I wanted. On the other hand, at least there was a possibility of a deep and meaningful relationship in the future with marriage and a family. They'll never happen with Annie. Annie told me she would be willing to go out with my friends once a month and see my family twice a month. I asked her why she willing to have sex with me if it doesn't do anything for her. She says knows that it would keep a man happy and is a good warm-up for when she gets home with Rod – that's what she calls her doll.

Now I have to decide – do I dump her or stay in a relationship that fulfills only some of my needs?

– Losing a Woman to A Doll

Dear Losing,

What your decision all boils down to is what you want out of the relationship in the long run. Cthulhu can assure you that I get letters from many men who would find what this woman is offering you to be the perfect relationship, but it seems like you may want something more meaningful. Some would recommend you give the relationship a try in the hopes that maybe you'll be able to convince her of your merits and that she will come to care for you, but not Cthulhu. Even if you managed to satisfy her once or twice, her doll's manufacturer will be coming out with upgrades and new models. You will never be able to keep up. And another thing to consider – since she is only dating you to please her mother, if anything happens to her mother, she will dump you immediately.

It seems as though the important part of the relationships to this this woman is having her physical needs met, while for you that it is only one of them.

Try the relationship for a few weeks and if you find that it's not enough to move on to greener pastures even if they're not as good-looking a pasture as this one.

Dear Cthulhu,

I'm a real man's man. At least I am to hear me tell it. There's not a sport I haven't played and mastered, at least when I'm out in the bars.

Truth is I never really played sports outside of gym in school, but the most important lesson I learned in high school is that girls like jocks. It didn't do me any good back then, but it has since. For one thing, after college, I moved a thousand miles away from my hometown, after first hitting up some thrift stores and picking up some letterman jackets. I regale everyone with the tales of how I was the quarterback of my high school football team and the starting pitcher for our baseball team.

Anytime there is any risk of someone asking me to join their work softball team or meet on Sunday for a game of two-hand touch, I sadly tell them of the "knee injury" that ended my imaginary athletic career back when I was a high school senior.

I'm smart and don't make the stories too outrageous, like I won state championships or something. Stuff like that shows up on the Internet and can be checked easily.

The lies really do work, especially with women who might suffer in the self-esteem department. Kind of the female version of myself. Believe it or not, there are a lot of girls out there who wanted to date a jock in high school and never had the opportunity. In that way, I feel I'm kind of doing a public service by filling an emotional need. The relationships never last long. I'd like to say it was because I got tired of the women and kicked them to the curb, but to be honest some of them were wonderful women. Once I helped bring their self-esteem up, they realized they could do better than me. That and once I started lying sometimes I had trouble stopping and eventually, people who spend more than a couple of hours a week with you will catch on.

One night at my favorite bar there was a beautiful woman who I tried to talk up. I had overheard part of a conversation and she didn't care much for team sports but loved boxing. I stepped up and regaled her with my brief but illustrious – and never before mentioned – high school boxing career. I was victorious in ten fights, two by knockout. I even put a draw and two losses in there to make it seem more realistic.

The woman could smell what I was shoveling and called me on it. I should've eavesdropped on the whole conversation before I started talking to her because she wasn't saying that she liked boxing. She was telling people that she was a professional boxer. "Punchy" called me a liar in front of everybody in the bar. And this was the bar where I spend most of my time. It was the one where I find most of the women who will actually date me. The bartender even cuts me a break on the drinks sometimes. I couldn't lose face, not there.

Like always, I had ended my story with how my knee injury had ended my athletic career. That's one thing I keep consistent. I always get the injury stealing and sliding into second base. Punchy wanted proof. I'd gotten quite good at Photoshop and offered to bring in a picture. That wasn't the kind of proof she wanted. She wanted a match between the two of us. Again I brought up my knee. Punchy told me it was no problem. She'd wrap up one of her knees so she couldn't bend it well and in the ring that would make us even.

I tried to go the gallant route and point out that I was five inches taller and fifty pounds heavier than she was. Punchy's response was to call me a sexist chicken, then she sweetened the pot. She said if I won, she'd go out with me for a month, but if she won I had to pay her bar tab for a month.

Either way, it was going to cost me money, either having to pay for her drinks or for all those dates. I wasn't sure what I was going to get out of it. I knew they'd be the kind of dates that ended with a handshake.

Then she did the chicken thing again and added flapping her arms and clucking. The rest of the bar started laughing so I had no choice but to agree to the match. I pointed out that

I hadn't boxed in years – not a lie since I'd never boxed at all. Punchy agreed to give me a month to train.

My question for you Cthulhu is, do you think I can do it? I've seen a bunch of boxing movies. There's always the training montage. I figure I'll find myself some wacky trainer or some old has-been boxer looking to redeem himself and they'll turn me into a lean, mean, fighting machine. The question is how do I find these kind of people? Is there a bar or club they hang out at? Should I invest in large hunks of meat to punch and train with? Or a way to get out of the whole fight? Please help me Cthulhu.

– Bigmouth Bragger in Bradford

Dear Bradford,

Like many braggarts and liars, you have put yourself in a position where you had to put up or shut up. Cthulhu is amazed by how many foolish humans won't just take a blow to their pride and shut up or back down. Now you have agreed to fight a professional boxer. It would be a mistake to think that you had an advantage just because of your size. Cthulhu has seen that it is a mistake to underestimate the determination and ferocity of the female of your species. Not to mention if she is a typical woman, she has had some – and possibly many – negative experiences with the males of your species. As a woman in a predominately male-dominated sport, Punchy has undoubtedly experienced much derision and had to train longer and harder than most male boxers. She will very likely be stepping into that ring and bringing with her that anger and resentment, all with the plan of unloading it all on you. Your best hope is to find yourself a decent trainer if you have the money. Do your best to get as good as you can in a short time. Since you were as least not foolish enough to claim to be a champion, if you at least make a decent showing, you will still lose but will have no reason to be embarrassed. In fact, after she kicks your posterior, be a gracious sportsperson and congratulate her. Punchy still won't likely date you, but perhaps she and the people from the bar who come to watch the fight may leave with some small measure of respect for you. And you will finally have a sports story that you don't have to lie about.

And no, I don't know of any benefits involved with training and hitting meat. Other than tenderizing it to eat later.

Of course, there other options. Tell the truth and apologize for lying. I sense that one will not appeal to you, but there is another possibility that would not involve training. Prior to this tie a tourniquet above and below the knee for an hour, but take them off before anyone can see them. You will risk an actual injury due to cutting off your blood supply, but it should cause some redness and swelling which will be crucial to the next step. On your way into the ring or as soon after you get in, twist your knee and fall to the ground screaming. Since it will look like an actual injury, it will likely get out of the match, but those watching will probably lose all respect for you as no matter how convincing you act. They will never fully believe that you were hurt. You will also not be able to return to your bar without much derision. These are your options, short of moving another thousand miles and starting over again. Whatever you decide, try and learn from your mistakes and develop skills that you can truthfully talk to females about.

Cthulhu Happens

Dear Cthulhu,

I am a fifteen-year-old boy and a sophomore in high school. I've haven't been on any dates, but I've been hoping to change that. There's this girl I really like and we've been flirting for a while. Yesterday as we were leaving lunch she leaned over and whispered in my ear that if I played my cards right she would go to second base with me.

Now I'll admit I didn't know it was a thing to go on dates at the baseball field, but I managed to find a deck of cards when my last class was over. I went out to the school baseball field and sat by second base. And I sat there and waited until after dark. "Abby" never showed and I got in trouble for missing dinner.

Abby seems like a nice girl. She's smart and pretty and funny. My insides tingle whenever I think of her. I thought maybe she felt the same way, but if that was true why didn't she show up for our date? Especially when she made it.

I'm too embarrassed to ask my buddies for advice because they're all much more experienced than me. Each one of them has gone all the way with at least one girl, although oddly the girls all live in different towns and rarely come to our town to visit. This is why I'm writing you.

– On and Off Base in Cooperstown

Dear Off,

First, as demonstrated by the previous letter, people lie so you should not feel too poorly because your exploits don't match up to those of your classmates. Their stories are probably fabrications and wishful thinking. If these boys are talking about their conquests with women who live far away, yet they're not old enough to drive, it is unlikely that they are true. They are most probably stories they tell to build up their own self-confidence and standing in your little circle. It is not an uncommon practice, but one that most people will grow out of, although not all.

As for your date with the young female – you misunderstood her. She wasn't telling you to meet her at second base. Human males love their sports analogies and have likened the sport of baseball to how far along the procreation trail they can get with the female of the species. There are some regional variations, but typically first base corresponds to kissing or making out. Second base is being able to touch the mammalian protuberances. Third-base is groping the posterior and below the waist. A home run is the act of procreation. Cleats need not be worn and bats should not be used. The young female was simply letting you know how far she was willing to let you go on a date. This, of course, means you should invite her on one. You seem like a reasonably decent fellow for human, so do it right. Ask her out, bring her flowers and take her somewhere nice, even if your parents have to drive you. Treat her like you would want to be treated and may have a long and fulfilling relationship. Do your best and give her no reason or cause to write to Dear Cthulhu about you. I'm busy enough as it is.

Dear Cthulhu,

I read your book *Cthulhu Know Best* with the letter from the girl who thought she had eaten unicorn meat with interest. I too have a young daughter "Uni" who too has been swept up with this unicorn-mania – unicorn posters, toys, video games, and movies. I thought it was cute until I came home drunk one night and called my wife by my mistress's name and got kicked out. As I was packing up a bag, my daughter was upset and crying. I had a headache from the booze and the beating my soon to be ex-wife gave me. I told Uni she could have anything she wanted if she would just stop crying. She asked for a real unicorn. I said fine just to make the noise stop – her crying sounds like someone put a cat and scrap metal in a blender and put it on puree. Let's just say it grated on my nerves.

When I got visitation with Uni the next weekend, the first thing out of her mouth was where was her unicorn. I barely remembered promising, but she had videoed me on the cell phone that we got her for her fifth birthday. My own kid threatened to sue me if I didn't deliver. My wife had already cleaned out all my bank accounts and I didn't have the money to pay for a lawyer and didn't want the embarrassment, so I started looking for a unicorn. There was nothing in the classifieds or on U-Bay, so I bought her a pony with my credit card. It was an old thing, barely able to walk and had to gum its hay, but was on its way to the dog food factory so I got it on the cheap.

I figured the pony would pacify her. I mean, even a six-year-old knows there is no such thing as a unicorn, right?

Wrong. The geezer pony wasn't good enough. She turned on her screechy voice and my head exploded. I made up some cock and bull story about unicorns having to camouflage themselves to survive in the modern world and that their horns now only came out on days where the moon is full.

Uni bought it. Unfortunately, she was also smart enough to do a web search and figure out the moon would be full on my next weekend with her.

I belong to a hunting lodge so I sawed off part of a gazelle horn from one of the trophy heads on the wall. Next, I tried to figure a way to attach it to the pony. Zany glue didn't do the trick and neither did Velcro. Duct tape worked but was kind of obvious.

The day before my daughter was due, I was desperate. I drilled a hole in the pony's forehead and put the horn in, securing it with the same epoxy people use for car body work. Even the part attached to his head was nice and shiny. But I'm no monster – I got the little guy drunk first.

Uni was thrilled; hugging and kissing the thing, even insisting it sleep in her bed. No screaming the entire weekend.

The problems started when Uni told her mother about the unicorn. The woman had the nerve to ask me if I had drilled a horn into a horse's head. Just because I did doesn't mean she should think so poorly of me that she'd ask after almost ten years of marriage. The woman called the ASPCA on me. Before they showed up, the pony's head started oozing green pus and the horn fell out. I took the little guy to the dog food factory and actually made a five-dollar profit.

When the ASPCA showed up, there was no pony or unicorn, so they left. What I'm worried about is what do I tell Uni? I don't want her to hate me or worse, start screeching.

-Missing a Unicorn in Mississippi

Dear Missing,

It is always nice to hear from someone who put his own selfish needs above those of other people and animals. I too have issues with the ASPCA over their definition of cruelty. They find it cruel that Cthulhu finds kittens with hollandaise sauce a delicacy. I find it cruel to deprive myself of such a delectable food.

The solution is simple and something you have already laid the groundwork for. You have told your daughter that unicorns have adapted to hide their horns to survive in the modern world. Simply tell her that when the animal inspectors – that her mother called – showed up the unicorn feared for its safety, fled, and will never return. Be sure to stress it was ultimately her mother's fault. It is a harsh lesson, but you should have cautioned the child about the possible consequences of telling others.

Dear Cthulhu,

My wife stopped having sex with me five and a half years ago. We've been married for six. I take my vows seriously, so I've never cheated on her, despite a couple of opportunities. Although to be honest, one of those was mainly because I didn't have the $2,000 and I'm afraid of ostriches.

Still, I'm a man with needs and online porn just wasn't cutting it anymore, so when "Frigina" began having trouble sleeping and her doctor gave her sleeping pills, I saw my opportunity. What's more, I took it and renewed our love life with interest for time lost. I was finally getting some, sometimes two times a night. Even better, with her asleep, I was finally able to try all the positions of the Kama Sutra book someone had given her for a wedding shower gift.

I was getting to do things I hadn't even dreamed of or heard about except on the porn sites that you have to pay for. I am getting to put my man part in places she never let me before. Although one time it almost backfired when her gag reflex got triggered and she bit down. That left a small scar, but otherwise, I was okay.

Frigina made it clear early on that children are like sex to her, something that could be tolerated on a rare occasion, but not something she wanted around her. I blame her strict religious upbringing. She grew up in a cult in which her father was the grand exalted leader and he messed her up bad.

Because of her views on kids, I used a condom at first. Who am I kidding? I knew she had taken the pill so it was mainly because I didn't want to get an STD. The more I thought about things, the more I realized that I really didn't need one for that. I was fairly certain I was her first partner, mainly because we met when I was counseling her after her father had been arrested along with the other cult leaders and put into jail. Our getting married ironically came out of me working to help her get past her dislike of sex by trying to prove that someone could think of her as a sexual object. Her father had the entire cult constantly tell her how unattractive she was and she eventually believed them. He also had all the women regale her with tales of how horrible sex was and it worked. Since she truly despises sex, I realized she'd never cheat on me so I stopped using the prophylactics.

Which may have been a mistake. Frigina felt nauseous and sick every morning for weeks. She went to the doctor and they gave her a pregnancy test. It was positive. She had no idea how it happened. I played dumb and demanded to know how it happened too and asked her about the birth control pills she took the first year were married. Turns out they only work for as long as you take them and she hadn't had any in years.

Not wanting her to catch on to what we were doing while she was asleep. I made my second mistake and said it was a miracle. Frigina took me literally and assumed it was some sort of divine birth. She even started telling people it was a virgin birth, despite my pointing out to her that because we had had sex those three times that she was no longer technically a virgin. She ignored me and is going to different churches and giving speeches and trying to get on the talk show circuit. So far no one is taking her seriously, but I worry someone might put her on just for the ha-ha factor.

What can I do to discourage this? And also, I'm not a monster. I don't want to harm our baby, so at what point in her pregnancy should I stop having nocturnal intercourse with Frigina?

And would it still be okay to continue to use her other orifices up to the actual birth?

– Nighttime Stud with a Muffin in the Oven

Dear Muffin,

You must not be a very effective counselor or you would realize what you're doing to your wife is not called sex, but is in fact rape. Not even Cthulhu can approve of your actions. It is wrong and must stop immediately. By human law, you should be in a jail cell.

Cthulhu also understands you would likely never tell her the entire truth as that would complicate matters for you, so I have contacted your wife to inform her what you have been doing. I also informed her as to how she got pregnant and that there was no mystic or divine infestation during procreation. If she chooses not to press charges or emasculate you while you sleep, perhaps the two of you should go to couples counseling with someone who is actually qualified to do the job. On the plus side for you, this should help stop her from making any further outrageous claims.

Neither of you seem like you would make good parents, so I suggest giving the child up for adoption. Or bring it to the zoo and let it be raised by wolves or meerkats so it will at least have a chance for a well-adjusted life.

Dear Cthulhu,

I read with interest a recent letter from a professional clown who got arrested because of the latest bigotry against those in the grease-face profession. I am in a similar situation.

I'm a professional clown named Mr. Bubbles and I've been doing children's parties since I was 14 years old. Admittedly, I'm a bit of the rebel. As my grades weren't good enough to get into Clown College, I went rogue. I'm mainly self-taught, although I have made a habit of going to the circus to study the greats. I'm a wizard at balloon animals and I can juggle just about anything that I'm strong enough to throw into the air and catch.

I've been making a living as a clown my whole adult life. It may not be glamorous and I may not be rich, but up until lately, I found it extremely fulfilling. True, there never seems to be enough birthdays in the winter but I tighten my big red belt, eat some ramen noodles, and manage to get by.

That all changed recently, thanks to my ex-girlfriend Giggles. She's a clown groupie. Admittedly, in my profession, the groupies can be hard to fight off sometimes. You'd be amazed how many bored housewives hire a clown for their kid's birthday party and then expect us to entertain them afterward in the bedroom. I'm only human and I admit that I'm more than one occasion I've succumbed to temptation. Admittedly, I usually get a big tip when I do that. I only charge $250 to do a party. The last time I entertained a mom, I got a $300 tip, but I have size 17 shoes in real life, so that helps attract the women.

I met Giggles at a six-year-old's birthday party. She wasn't the mom that hired me. In fact, she wasn't even invited. She heard I was coming and crashed the party. She waited in line until all the kids were done and then asked me to make a balloon animal of myself. I obliged and then with her back to the rest of the party, Giggles began to use her hands to do all sorts of unspeakable things to the inflatable me. It was oddly hot and I was lucky I was wearing baggy pants.

When the party was done, Giggles was waiting outside to offer me a ride – as a clown I utilize public transportation as I don't really make enough to pay for a car or the insurance.

As I looked inside the car, she had her skirt hiked up and her blouse unbuttoned down to her navel. I told her sure and got in, Giggles gave me a ride down to the nearest Lovers' Lane where she gave me a ride of a whole different sort. We dated for months. The woman was a super freak. I mean I live the life, but even I never thought of half the uses she came up with for cream pies and rubber chickens.

Things were great for a while but then, like in any relationship, who we are starts to show through the veneer of who we pretend to be something. Things started to unravel. She realized that I was a bit of a slob and I realized she was a twisted psychotic.

I broke up with Giggles, but it turned out to be no laughing matter. She didn't take it well. I went with the whole it is not you, it's me. Turns out she bought it and decided to punish me by making my life a living hell.

Giggles destroyed my apartment. Everything I have from my TV to my furniture was all secondhand. She destroyed it all with an ax and a live skunk she must've caught the woods somewhere. Worse than stinking up my home, Giggles shredded all my clown clothes and wigs then flushed my makeup down the toilet. Worst of all, she cut up a red nose that I had bought on U-Bay that had once belonged to the legendary Emmett Kelly.

The only bright spot in the whole mess was that I actually had renter's insurance – a guy hired me to do three of his kids' parties and didn't want to pay me. Turns out he sold insurance and offered me a three-year policy instead. As it had already been six months when he made that offer and I hadn't gotten a dime, I figured it was better than nothing. I ended up getting all new furniture, an HDTV, and new locks for all the doors and windows. It even paid for me to upgrade my clown gear, although the Emmett Kelly nose was irreplaceable.

Then one night I woke up to see her staring in at me from my bedroom window, which was kind of freaky since I live on the third floor and there's no fire escape.

Next, I got inundated with jobs, in the winter no less. That should've been my first clue that something was wrong. I have my website set up to book parties, so I don't necessarily talk to the people who are hiring me.

The first job was supposed to be a birthday party for a five-year-old girl and it turned out to be a getting out of jail party for a member of a biker gang. I thought I was dead, but after they checked me to make sure I wasn't wearing a wire, I did my shtick for a triple murderer who had just gotten out of the penitentiary. Spike thought it was hilarious. Seems he'd told his biker buddies a sad story about when he was a kid and the clown he was expecting never came to his birthday party. Spike actually cried that they remembered and cared enough to get a clown for this party. I learned that not only can I make balloon animals, but balloon motorcycles and guns. I ended up being made a member of the gang, mainly based on my unicycle skills. My gang name is the Bubblenator.

For the next job, I ended up at a bingo game in a retirement community and the ladies there didn't appreciate me interrupting their game or juggling the bingo balls and ended up beating me senseless with their canes and purses. The old biddies sent me to the emergency room.

Then it got worse. Giggles must've hacked my website and found when I had legitimate jobs, then called 911 and reported a creepy clown lurking about, so when I wound up arriving at the children's parties, the cops were waiting. Parents are not thrilled when the person they hired to entertain at their kid's party is seen sitting in the back of a police car while the officer sorts everything out. Every single family canceled my appearance. I even got arrested once and spent the night in jail because a cop had a fear of clowns and used me to physically work through it.

I ended up being let go in the morning but I can't go on like this.

Giggles is crippling my ability to make a living. I complained to the cops each time that she was harassing me, but apparently, she used a burner phone and a voice modulator to make the 911 calls, so they're not able to prove that she actually did anything.

To add to my misery my main clown rival, Colonel Laughter – believe me, he's more like canned laughter – has been getting all the jobs that would normally have gone to me and it's making me nuts. We used to be friends back in high school. In fact, I took him under my wing and taught him everything he knows about clowning. I even had him do parties with me for a couple years, but then he decides he doesn't need me and betrayed me by trying to steal my customers. It burns me up that he may actually end up coming out on top, especially since he's a no talent hack who just recycles what I was doing ten years ago.

I'm at my wit's end. I'm afraid I'll have to get a normal job which will thrill my dad to no end. He's always wanted me to work for him and take over his drywall company. What can I do to stop Giggles?

– A Clown Who Doesn't Think This Is Funny Anymore In Anaheim

Dear Anaheim,

It sounds like your ex-girlfriend does indeed have many psychological issues and that she is actually quite devious and intelligent. From your description in your letter, you really have no chance of beating her in a head-on competition. I don't think you have it in you to lay a trap to catch her at her own game, so I see two options available for you. The first is to get back together with her. Yes, it will be a challenging relationship for you to navigate, but it does sound as if at least the procreational component of your relationship was fulfilling. For many males of your species that is enough to make them endure a lot. Do that and she will stop her attacks upon your livelihood and you will be able to do what you love.

The better option would be to meet with Giggles and tell her that she's won and that you are retiring from the clown business. And tell her that she deserves a better man than you, the best clown in town. Then point her at this Colonel Laughter. With her clown fetish, it shouldn't take her too long to turn her sights on him instead of you. Then you need only wait for things to follow the same path they did with you and her attentions will turn to your rival, you will be able to return to your life of clowning. If they break up, Giggles will turn all her revenge notions on him should break up. In the meantime, make your father happy by working for him for a short time doing drywall. Plus, it gives you some job skills to fall back on.

Dear Cthulhu,

It turns out they've been having a bullying problem at my child's school. I've been getting notes from the principal about it for weeks. Then I was called in for a conference with his teacher and the principal. Imagine my shock and dismay when I learned that the bully was none other than my own son. I mean, I knew he had issues after his mother ran off and left us to join the professional bodybuilder and cooking circuit. I miss her too; especially the times and she'd bench press me during sex while she made a chocolate soufflé.

And it didn't help matters when Junior got into the stash of anabolic steroids his mother left behind. Junior began to look like a 4-foot version of the Incredible Hulk, minus the green skin. I had pretended to ignore it because Junior misses his mommy and his taking her pills made him feel closer to her.

Turns out he's been having anger issues and beating up the other kids at school. I sat him down so we could have a father-son chat and I explained that bullying and beating up weaker people was wrong. He responded by wrestling me to the ground, stealing my wallet, and giving me a wedgie.

I later learned he would've been suspended earlier except he had beaten up his teacher and she was afraid of him too.

I don't seem to be getting through to Junior and he seems so angry all the time. I'm worried if this keeps up that he won't make it into the third grade. What can I do?

– Pounded Poppa in Poughkeepsie

Dear Pounded,

Anabolic steroids are not intended for a human whom Cthulhu surmises must be about eight years of age. Even on adult humans, they have been shown to have various negative side effects, not the least of which is something called roid rage. The first thing you should do find all the steroids and destroy them. Next, take your son to a competent physician and get him a full checkup. Perhaps even have him talk to a guidance counselor at the school about issues dealing with his mother's abandonment of her family. Do all this and in a few months, the situation should be more under control as his body returns to normal.

In the meantime, take a page from your wife's book and start working out. There is no way a man, even a tiny one, should be beaten up by an eight-year-old.

That or – as long as you do not mind the devastating long term effects of steroids on a child – consider pitching a show about child professional wrestlers – call it CPW. It will give your offspring a place to work off his roid rage and earn some money for college.

DEAR CTHULHU™

Dear Cthulhu,

I've recently begun playing Knight Qwest. It's part online/part live action role playing game divided up into kingdom zones, usually by city. People pretend they are going out on quests in order to earn knighthood and other titles. The quests are often scavenger hunts and the like. Businesses pay to have the players come to their store or restaurant. They play up the knight angle up and the gamers usually end up buying an item or dinner or some such. For each completed quest, they get codes which they can use to unlock the next level online which unlocks more quests in the real world.

For a gimmick, they placed a sword in a stone in each kingdom zone, the idea being that the players would work harder to do more quests to get enough points to be the first to unlock the sword and become king of the zone for a year.

I play KQ and as luck would have it my cousin's employer was hired to install the swords. He was hung over and asked me to fill in for him. We kinda look alike and we'd done it before so I went. It took about six hours. The player is supposed to wave their smart phone with their player ID on the screen – it's one of those funky new bar code things – near a scanner. Then it decides if the player has enough points to release the clamp on the sword and allow them to become king of all England or, in my case, Cleveland.

We also installed a special quest prize on the side of the stone that had enough points to allow whoever solved the puzzle to open the side of the stone and scan that code, which would automatically give them enough points to pull out the sword.

It was an incredibly difficult puzzle that would probably give someone like Einstein or Hawkings trouble. Of course, since I installed it, figuring it out was a bit easier.

The restaurant that was sponsoring the stone and the sword threw in a free meal a week for the year's reign, the idea being the king would hold court there and all the other players would come and pay for their meals. And it was on Tuesdays, which I guess is a traditionally slow night for eating out.

They held a big premier party. The idea was that every Tuesday players would come and try to pull the sword. Getting points the regular way would make the process take months or longer. I went with friends and we watched as everyone scanned their player code and tried to pull the sword. It didn't budge.

Finally, it was my turn. A lot of people had tried the puzzle, but only I solved it. I scanned the code to my account, then put my smart phone in front of the scanner. Dramatically I put my hands on the hilt and pulled. It slid out and I raised it over my head to the applause of the other players.

I was crowned Calvin I, King of all Cleveland. It was the greatest moment of my life. But it got better. Apparently being king in Knight Qwest actually came with some power. I had a certain amount of points that I could bestow each week and the hardcore players were willing to do a lot to get them. Guys were offering me video games and cash, but the ladies were willing to offer more. I could knight one player a week and found out quickly that some women were willing to trade a night at my place in exchange for the rank. I'm not normally a babe magnet and my last steady girlfriend was back in college, so I was happy to make the exchange.

Then a rep from the game sent out an e-mail to all the players in the zone that I as king could appoint other royalty – a baron and baroness, count and countess, duke and duchess and lastly a queen.

I got an old but running used convertible for the dukedom, but there were three ladies who really wanted to be queen. Two of them came onto me right after that royal court, each promising me more carnal pleasures than the other. The whole king thing had been going to my head, so I proposed a competition to prove who would do more. They both came back to my place and competed together, each trying to prove her case, sometimes pulling the other off so they could get to me. They meant it when they said they'd do anything. I went through all my fantasies inside of three days and had to start trolling online porn for more ideas. And they did each of them. Repeatedly.

Then after the next royal court, another woman got into the act. She wasn't willing to do what the other two were or with them, but she was much prettier.

I'm in heaven. Mel Brooks was right – it is good to be king. So what's my problem you ask? The game mandates I hand out the titles by the end of the month. I have no delusions. I know this female attention will stop the moment I appoint the royal titles.

How do I make it last longer? By the rules of the game, I can't be king again for two years. And what the ladies are willing to do for a knighthood is nowhere near what they're willing to do to be queen.

Neither of the freaky girls is great looking, but they've been great sports. The pretty one kind of just lays there and plays Knight Qwest while we're doing it, but if I picked her she'd be sitting next to me during all the royal courts and photo ops, making me look good. Who should I pick?

-King Calvin I of Cleveland

Dear Calvin,

First up, very impressive showing in turning a meaningless game into a way to fulfill your procreation fantasies.

Second and more importantly, do not expect to be addressed as your majesty – there is only one destined ruler of humanity and that is Cthulhu.

You are correct in that the chances of prolonging your royal benefits are slim, so I recommend you taking advantage of them as much as possible in the time you have left.

As for whom to make queen, Cthulhu prefers to reward effort, so I would grant the more attractive female the lesser title.

Cthulhu does see an outside chance of prolonging the benefits if you follow this plan. Are either of the remaining ladies easier to fool than the other? If so, make a document that appears to be from the game company and make up a list of queenly duties. Mark it as secret. Take a page from your own government's national security oaths. Before showing her the queen duties, make her sign a "Knight Qwest" security oath that states if she either reveals the contents of the document or fails to fulfill her duties, or even discusses it with an employee of the company, that she can be removed from the office of queen and exiled from the game forever. If they are that intent on playing this nonsense, this might be enough to make them continue. Then simply list taking care of the king's royal procreation needs as one of the duties. Don't put an expiration date on it and maybe when you year reign if done, you can still hold the exile portion over her head. Perhaps even try it for the other one to give her a royal title as well.

Dear Cthulhu,

I'm a member of a group of cosplayers. We started out dressing like anime and manga characters but have since branched out. Lately, we've been going with lots of steampunk – you know, 1800's era inspired clothing, especially the hats, not to mention lots of goggles thrown in for good measure. Dressing up in costume is something I've always enjoyed doing, but it does mark me as a geek. Not that there's anything wrong with it, except when it comes to meeting women. Well, the meeting part is easy. It's the getting them to go out with me that's hard.

I was going to be at a convention and wanted to try out some new gimmicks I had, including a smoke bomb that would fill up a small portion of the hallway, so I could make a dramatic entrance by walking through it. I went to the hotel a week early to see what hallway would work best. I wanted to check the lighting, make sure the ventilation system wouldn't get rid of the smoke too quickly, that kind of thing. There was no convention then, but there was a wedding. I set off the smoke bomb and walked through it, only to come out and find myself facing a gorgeous and drunk bridesmaid.

She took one look at me and asked if I was a time traveler. I figured it was due to the old-time clothing, so I told her yes. For some reason, she then assumed that I was from the future instead of the past, despite my garb. I didn't argue because a pretty girl was talking to me. Then Bridesmaid asked me if I was here to save the world. I told her yes I was. This apparently got her extremely hot and she took me back to her room in the hotel where she got rid of her dress and made a lot of my fantasies come true. She even let me keep my goggles and hat on.

I got her number and called her the next day. To be honest, I was more than a little worried that she wouldn't be interested in me once she sobered up. I made my peace with it because I had never had a one-night stand that I could brag about before. There was this one time in college I woke up with a woman in bed next to me, but there was an ostrich too and it was all part of some sort of sorority initiation.

Turns out that Bridesmaid was still interested in me. Even sober, she wasn't the fastest gear in the works. She still believed I was a time traveler from the future. However, she was hot to trot and we did it every day that week. When Friday came I went to my convention, telling her it was part of my mission. I made the mistake of telling my friend Bart. Like me, he's a cosplayer, but where I always dressed as a hero, he always goes as a villain. Bart didn't believe me, so at the end of the convention, I let him follow me to Bridesmaid's apartment. I went in and spent the night. Bart stayed in his car outside until I left the next morning. Then he went up to Bridesmaid's door and knocked. When she answered, the scumbag told her he was also from the future and was sent to stop me and ensure that evil triumphed. Turns out Bridesmaid is more into bad boys because she jumped his bones and shut me out.

I realize it's partially my fault for bragging, but it ticks me off that Bart has her and I don't. I'm tempted to tell Bridesmaid the truth. If I do, do you think she'll dump Bart? And you think there's a chance she might take me back because she was so impressed with my honesty?

– Real Cosplayer and Fake Time Traveler in Cincinnati.

Dear Cosplayer,

It has been Cthulhu's experience that honesty is rarely the best policy. The odds of this woman wanting to procreate with you again after finding out she's been lied to by not one, but two men, are so minimal as to not be worthy of consideration. The fact that her own gullibility contributed to it won't make a difference. Her anger toward you for having fooled her will far exceed any gratitude she may have over being told the truth.

Since the woman is so gullible, why not simply add to your back story? Go to her while she is with Bart, use one of your smoke bombs and emerge laughing maniacally. Thank her profusely for distracting Bart and allowing you to complete your mission to destroy the future. Tell her that Bart was really the good guy masquerading as the bad guy, while you were the bad guy masquerading as the good guy and now the future that you both came from has been forever destroyed and replaced with a dark and evil one. Then turn and slowly walk away. She will likely yell at your friend Bart for lying to her, perhaps dump him. There is an outside chance she may even come after you to replace him in her bed. And even if the last part does not happen, at least you've sabotaged Bart's procreation with your former bed partner.

Dear Cthulhu,

I recently wrote to you about my girlfriend cheating on me with a Japanese sex robot doll she calls "Rod". I decided to ride it out with Dolly, so to speak, mainly because I lost my job and my apartment and she let me move in with her and Rod. The problem is that she is constantly carrying on with Rod and I can't get any sleep what with the screaming and mechanical whirling but I don't want to be homeless. I can't compete with what this stupid sex robot does to her. The only time I get any is before and after we have to see her mother. She parades me around in front of her so Mom doesn't get bothered about her not having a boyfriend.

To be honest, if I were rich like Dolly I'd get a female version of the doll for myself, but I can barely afford a pizza let alone the six figures the base model costs.

While she was at work, Dolly told me to install Rod's software update. I figured maybe I could program him for less impressive acts so she will give me a try more often. The choices were between software for Rod and Dorothy. I figured Dorothy was the mode for women who just wanted a friend to cuddle with.

Boy, was I wrong.

Rod woke up and came after me. Apparently, I mistook the preferred roughness setting and picked the lowest, which was actually the highest. Rod did things to me that I've never experienced and never want to again. Oddly enough, he cuddled afterwards.

Now Rod appears to be in love with me and Dolly is furious at me for stealing her sexbot. Believe you me, I don't want him or the bruises he left on me. I convinced her to give me another go. Rod saw it and is now curled up into a ball in the corner weeping. Dolly is weeping in another corner.

What am I going to do?

– Losing a Woman to a Doll Who Wants Me

Dear Losing,

First off, reinstall the update under the Rod setting. "Dorothy" is part of an old-time signal from a less enlightened time when gay men had to ask each other if they were "friends of Dorothy" to identify each other. Certainly, you do not think just women buy these procreation bots?

Next, call the company that makes Rod and inform them of your traumatizing assault by their product. Lie and tell them your girlfriend recorded it. Tell them you will not release it to the public if they will supply you with a female procreation robot of your own. This way you will stop whining and get some robotic procreating of your own done.

Dear Cthulhu,

I've always wanted to be a Peeping Tom, but I was always afraid of getting caught, so I never had the guts to do it until recently. Although technically I guess I'd be a Peeping Thomasina being a woman and all.

I was at a steam punk convention where they were selling foil dirigibles – blimps for non-steam punkers. They were silver, more than three feet long and came with remote controls. They were pretty neat to play with, so I bought one.

Then I came up with the brilliant idea of hooking up a wireless high-definition camera to it. I live next door to an incredibly hot guy, a real hard body type. I saw him once outside getting a tan and had to run inside to use my adult toys.

After I got the camera set up, I waited until it was dark and opened up an upstairs window that was over my backyard and sent my airship out on its first reconnaissance mission. The hi-def camera had an infrared mode, so I was able to maneuver it in the dark. First, I had it fly by Hottie's bathroom window and lucked out because he was just getting undressed for the shower. The steam fogged up the shower glass, blocking much of the actual action, but the before-and-after shots were pretty amazing. Next, he went into the bedroom. It turns out he sleeps in the all-together. Jackpot! Especially when he did his naked calisthenics. Hubba hubba. Momma's toys got a good workout that night, believe you me.

This went on for a week until Hottie looked out the window and saw my airship. He screamed and I did evasive maneuvers, bringing the airship high up above the houses and back down and through my back window. He didn't see where it went and it got away clean.

The next night my fun was over. Hottie had gotten curtains for all the windows. I thought my peep time was over. I had recorded everything, but I already knew what was going to happen so it just wasn't the same.

The next day I bumped into him as we were taking out our garbage cans to the curb like we had a dozen times before. Planned of course. I kept spare garbage nearby at all times just in case.

Hottie said hi like usual but then actually talked to me for the first time beyond a simple hello or good bye. Turns out he thought my airship was a government drone sent to spy on him. Turns out Hottie was a sales rep for a drug company and had a side business selling narcotics and other street drugs. He replaces the samples with breath mints and the like. He thought the government was after him and thought he was going to have to move out.

That was the last thing I wanted, so I got up the courage to offer to let him come stay with me for a couple of nights. And Hottie took me up on it. I barely had enough time to get pin hole cameras set up in my bathroom and shower before he got there, not to mention my extra bedroom.

Those shots were incredible, up close and personal, almost like I was there and could reach out and touch him. After a couple nights, Hottie offered me a couple of bucks, but I refused so he made a counter proposition. Hottie offered me pharmaceuticals. I took a couple narcotics and ground them into his protein shake. I mixed in some male potency pills. A few sips and gulps later, he was high and busting out of his jeans. It didn't take much to seduce him – he had actually started humping my stove. I slid right in and he kept on going. We did it right there in my kitchen. And then in my bedroom and finally in the shower, all caught in glorious full color on my hidden camera there.

Problem is the next day he didn't come back or call and I wanted him to come back desperately. He was so much better than my toys. How can I get Hottie back into my camera range again?

-Peeping Thomasina in Tonawanda.

Dear Peeping,

Loving and leaving may actually be his standard operating procedure. Many men only want procreation, nothing more, and don't like to repeat themselves with the same partners or let things like emotions or personal morals guide their conduct.

Arrange to meet him at the garbage cans again and casually mention that you have seen a sedan with two guys in suits in it parked across from his house at odd hours of the day and night and it looked like they were taking pictures. And a deliveryman knocked on his door and went inside for twenty minutes without coming out. He'll think the authorities have a search warrant and bugged his house to watch and listen. Again offer your home as a hide out. Maybe you will be able to procreate with him without having to resort to drugging him. And if that doesn't work, at least you'll have more shower videos of him to add to your collection.

Dear Cthulhu,

I'm a woman who lives in a big city. I moved here for a job and I haven't made many friends yet. I'm just out of college and I don't make a lot of money, so I have to take the subway to work every day. I didn't use to mind, but recently something has changed.

There's a guy who's been bothering me on the train. I thought it was weird how he always seems to end up standing next to me. I don't know many people in the city so I figured I'd say hi, maybe strike up a conversation and meet someone new. I thought he must have been shyer than me because he barely managed to whisper hi and the conversation didn't progress past that. As the week went on he started standing closer to me, rubbing up against my back or my front. In a crowded subway car at rush-hour that's not too uncommon so didn't think too much of it until one day when I felt his hand grab my butt. I was so shocked I froze and things got worse as he kept doing it. I tried to move away from him, but he followed me.

I started taking trains at different times, but he always seemed to get on my train and in the same car. It progressed to the point where he started grinding against me. I was afraid and ashamed so I just stood there and tried to ignore it as best I could. I looked around at the other passengers hoping to find someone to help me, but they were all too busy reading the paper or texting or talking on their phones to notice what was happening to me, so I stood there and did my best to ignore it until my subway stop came.

For the first time, he got off at my stop. I sprinted up the stairs and down the street and he didn't follow.

That was Thursday. I called in sick to work on Friday but I'm really worried about what's going to happen on Monday. The buses don't go anywhere near work. I can't afford a cab and it's too far to walk.

What should I do?

-Frightened On the Subway

Cthulhu Happens

Dear Frightened,

The first and best thing Cthulhu can recommend to you is to cease being a victim. No other human has the right to touch or otherwise assault you against your will. It is one of the rights Cthulhu grants you. This lowlife predator got bolder because you ignored his first assaults.

There are several ways to handle this. You could report him to your local police force. The truth of it, however, is most police departments are understaffed and overworked. Without any other witnesses, it would be your word against his word. Unfortunately for you, the criminal justice system in your country is still often skewed and tries to place some blame on the woman for these kind of assaults. And oddly many of these same people who do this would consider Cthulhu evil.

You might be able to get an order of protection, but the value of that is limited by how well the predator follows it. Of course, the police could do an undercover sting operation, but the odds of them doing that for what *they* would consider a simple groping are minimal. You stand a better chance of winning a lottery.

Do you have a group of friends or co-worker who could ride with you? There can be safety in numbers.

This predator appears to be counting on you being too embarrassed to do anything to stop him. Turn the tables. The next time he tries to assault you, be loud and make a scene. Bring attention to what he is doing. Embarrass him. Yell things like "Why is your hand on my buttocks?" or "Why are you grinding up against me?" Loudly demand that he stop. Do not be embarrassed as you have done nothing wrong. All fault is his.

Film him with your cellphone. Suggest others riding with you do the same. Although from his chosen method of attack he appears to be a coward, there is no guarantee that he will not resort to violence, so do not do anything you do not think you can handle.

Of course, even if this makes him go away, this poor excuse

for a human may still prey on other women. A moment of embarrassment is hardly a real punishment for his assaults on your person and the fear he had caused you. In an ideal world, the only one you should fear is Cthulhu himself. Alas, you humans prevent this world from being ideal.

The preferred option of Cthulhu is to punish the wrong doer and to enjoy one's self when doing it. Purchase a handheld stun gun. Like many dangerous things, they are available on the Internet. It is powered by a nine-volt battery. When you return to the subway, pull your hand up into the sleeve of your coat and hide the stun gun. When this poor excuse for a human starts his attack on your person, place the stun gun up against him - perhaps even the same area he is grinding against you - and press the button. Repeatedly. This will likely knock him to his knees, so it would be best to wait until you are near a subway stop. Do it just before the train halts and then get off. That way you are less likely to be caught by law enforcement for defending yourself. If you are caught, tell them the truth about what has been happening, making sure to weep and sob. This will likely help your case as humans seem to feel worse for their fellow humans that do this. With luck, you will be let off with a warning. Or if filmed by your fellow passengers, become a viral sensation for a being a female bold enough to put a predatory male down in his place.

At the very least, this poor excuse for a human will likely reconsider assaulting any more women.

Dear Cthulhu,

I started at my company five years ago - believe it or not - in the mailroom. I was never popular in high school or college and learned to get by without people. I mean I have family and they're okay. At least I can tolerate them in small doses around the holidays.

Because of my lack of a social life, I really don't have much problem working 80 hours a week, which helps explain how I became the youngest vice president in my company's history. Of course, sometimes I was lonely but I have lots of money and was able to buy companionship, if you know what I mean.

My sister was worried about me and for my birthday bought me a puppy. At first, I thought it was a horrible gift. I was going to take it to an animal shelter the next day, but then the little guy climbed up into my lap and licked my face. I started to pet him. I fell asleep with the dog next to me and by the next morning I decided to keep "Runt".

Over the next few weeks, a strange thing happened. I had more to look forward to than just work. I actually stopped going into the office on weekends. I left work by 8 o'clock instead of 10, so I'd have time to go home and take Runt for a walk, then play with him before going to bed. I hired a dog walker to take him out while I was at work.

I finally had something that money couldn't buy, love and companionship. Not that there's anything freaky between me and the dog. Well, there was that one night that I came home drunk and woke up with peanut butter in embarrassing places, but that's something the dog and I are doing our best to pretend never happened.

All was well until my dog walker went off and joined the Occupy the Coffee Party movement. That meant I had to hire another one. I picked the nicest one with the best references, which may have been the biggest mistake of my life. It was a senior citizen who was living on her pension and looking for some supplemental income. Apparently, she had too much time on her hands and decided to spend most of it with my dog. Instead of just walking him, she took him out to play for hours at the dog park. She cooked him homemade meals and knitted him sweaters. Now Runt seems happier to see the old lady then he does me. By the time I get home from work he's too tired to go for a long walk and he barely wants to play.

What it boils down to is I think my dog loves his dog walker more than he does me. And it's driving me crazy. Am I just being paranoid? Would it be wrong of me to set some boundaries about what she can and cannot do with my dog? A dog is supposed to love its owner more than anybody else right? Isn't a rule or a law or something?

I met a guy at a conference who claims he knows people that will knock off somebody else for a few grand. Would it be wrong of me to put a hit out on this woman so I have my dog all to myself again?

– Aggravated Doggie Daddy in Denver

Dear Denver,

No, you are not being paranoid. Cthulhu gets a multitude of letters from people whose loved ones' affection has been alienated from them and given to another. True, usually it is a spouse or significant other, but the principle is the same. I also get letters from the people who do the moving on. They tell me about how their former loved one doesn't spend time with them anymore. One of the more common reasons is because they are too busy with work. Most of these people tell Cthulhu that the person that they cheat with is not necessarily better looking or more skilled at procreation. It simply a matter of them being willing to spend time with them and lavish them with at least the illusion of affection. It is important for most humans to feel as though somebody cares about them.

The same appears to have happened with you and your dog. By your own admission, even though you have cut down the number of hours you spend earning a living, you still devote the majority of your time to your job while this woman spends most of hers with the canine. It is only natural that the pair would form a bond. And since she spends more time, it stands to reason their bond would be stronger.

As to whether or not you should hire others to end the woman's life, Cthulhu says no. Cthulhu's position on humans killing other humans remains unchanged. All humanity will one day be the property of Cthulhu and no one other than Cthulhu has the right to destroy Cthulhu's property.

There is a much easier solution that you are overlooking. Simply fire the woman and hire another dog walker, preferably a professional who has a number of clients whose dogs get walked at the same time. This ensures that your dog gets some socialization with other of its kind, but that neither he nor the dog walker will get overly attached to each other.

Then you can slowly begin the task of rebuilding a relationship with your canine. You mentioned working many hours, but you do not mention anything about taking vacations. There are places that will cater to holidays specifically for people and their pets. Look into one and take some time off and go. Then once a month, take a day or half a day off and come home to spend time with your dog. Look into the option of telecommuting. Are there any of your duties that could be done from home? If this is possible you would be able to work and be with the dog at the same time.

If this does not work and your dog refuses to return your affections to your satisfaction, remember the dog is a lower life form as compared to you, much like humans are to Cthulhu. That gives you the right to decide whether it lives or dies. And if you decide to end its existence, might Cthulhu recommend doing so by way of barbecue. While not as tasty as kitten, dog roasted on a spit with some rosemary and sage can be quite a delicacy. Then you can simply get another dog and start over. Or – because PETA will be upset with my last recommendation – you could consider gifting the dog to the old woman and simply getting a new one for yourself. Or if you decide to go with the first option, invite the old woman over for a barbecue dinner. I doubt she will be bonding with anyone else's pet after that.

Dear Cthulhu,

Me again – the guy whose girlfriend cheated on him with a sex robot. I followed your advice and the robot company gave me my own sex robot – Floozette – and things were great. I had amazing sex with her. She did things so much better than Dolly and some things Dolly would never do, not even with Rod. The puree setting is amazing. I needed to soak in the tub for an hour before I could walk right again.

With my new confidence, I got another job at twice the money. Now Dolly and I are both pretending to be the other's significant other to make our families happy.

Everything was like a dream until I got the not-so-bright idea of us having a foursome with the robots. It went well, the robots even engaging with each other.

The next day, we both came home to hear the mechanical buzzing and whirling of the sexbots. My first thought is someone had broken in and was having sex with Floozette or Rod. It was worse than that – the robots were having sex with each other!

We tried to pull them apart and make them stop but they ignored us and kept at it all night in Dolly's room so she had to bunk with me. Worse, she made me sleep on the floor instead of loving the one she was with.

They hadn't stopped when we left for work the next day. I don't know what to do. Apparently, since the sex is so much better with the sexbots they have decided to ignore the humans in the apartment in favor of each other. Neither of us is happy and Dolly is blaming me.

How can I fix this and get my sexy Floozette interested in me again?

– Losing another Woman/Sexbot to a Doll

Dear Losing,

There is a simple solution. Wait until the robots' batteries run out – make sure to take the recharging cords out of the apartment – and when they turn off, reset both to factory settings. This should erase their memories of each other. Then make sure to never allow them to have contact with each other again. And to be on the safe side, turn them off when you leave the apartment.

Dear Cthulhu,

I am a writer who has spent at least thirty to forty minutes every month for the last year dedicated to my craft. I have started over fifty novels and one day I hope to finish at least one of them. In the meantime, I've tried my hand at poetry and short story writing.

Sadly, the world has yet to recognize my brilliance. I feel a very large part of my lack of success as a writer stems from that failure. That lack of recognition of my genus is to be blamed for my not completing anything. Because – and let's be honest here – the moment the masses bow down in the praise I deserve, I'd have the encouragement and motivation I need to finish one of my epic works. Maybe even two. I mean, it's not easy to write and still have a job and a social life.

The latest in the long line of those not recognizing my literary mastery is David Lee Summers, the editor of that rag *Tales of the Talisman*. I liked what I read in his magazine and figured this guy might have something on the ball so I sent him one of my unfinished novels about how Christopher Columbus really used nanotechnology in a ghost bus built from chocolate pudding and sunbeams to discover the hidden city of Newark and covered it all up by saying he discovered America in order to prevent an invasion of alien cyborg llamas that were harvesting humans for their tasty uvulas.

As soon as I got Summer's reply, I lost all respect for the man. First off, he told me he expected me to read his writer submission guidelines, obviously not understanding that someone as special as I am is exempt –nay – beyond any artificial construction such as a man-made restriction on brilliance.

Then he goes on to tell me that the magazine doesn't publish novels, particularly unfinished ones. Then he complains that he thought it was difficult to read because I "accidentally" assembled the chapters in a random order without any numbering. Let me tell you, that was no accident. That was *brilliance*. A true reader or editor would realize that and simply read the whole book at least once, then go back and try and assemble the chapters in the right order just to be a part of my greatness. Didn't he see Pulp Fiction? That didn't go in order. And this is even more brilliant because even though that movie didn't go in order, it was at least put in a sequence where it could be understood by the viewer. My novel wasn't challenged by any such limitation. I figured Summers could publish it before it was finished and then I would arbitrarily place the final chapters on different Internet sites and stapled to telephone poles on random street corners for my hordes of fans to find on their own.

I wrote this so-called editor back and explained him in no uncertain terms about how wrong he was, about how shortsighted his thinking is and that he wouldn't know art if it bit him in the butt. Not that I would do such a thing – my real name is actually Art, short for Arturo although I hadn't decided for sure if I would write under that name. It seemed too plebeian. I'm thinking Fluffy McBoomroom XIX.

However, I'm not an unreasonable man so I gave Summers another chance and sent him three more of my novels. This time he complained that my submission made even less sense because I had randomly mixed the chapters from not just one but three different unfinished works. Summers again failed to see the *genius* of what I did. Can you imagine the reaction when people realize they got not just one, but three novels that would allow them the joy of searching and figuring out not just what order the chapters went in, but to what novel? People would be thrilled by the novelty and they'd be excited because they got three for the price of one. Summers wrote back again, once more going on about these writer's guidelines and the importance of following them if I wanted to be published in his little rag.

Truth be told, I am partially to blame. One time shame on you, two times shame on me. I shouldn't have given him a second chance. Still, I'm having trouble letting it go. Then I noticed that you appeared in nineteen of the last twenty issues. I figured the reason you didn't appear in the one was you probably had some sort of beef with this editor as well, so you'd understand where I was coming from. Would you speak to this David Lee Summers and point out what an imbecile he's being? Then tell him that he needs to publish my work. And let him know I won't take less than a half million dollars as an advance, but he can pay half on acceptance and half on publication.

– Artful Author in Albuquerque (aka Fluffy McBoomroom XIX)

Dear Artful,

    Cthulhu is continually amazed at the ability of so many hum'ans to refuse to accept responsibility for their own actions or to blame their failures on others. Cthulhu is not going to lie to you and tell you that this David Lee Summers is the greatest editor who ever lived. He is not. However, he is better than most, if for no other reason than his good sense to carry the Dear Cthulhu column. The man is only human – which is not meant as a compliment by any means – and only has so much time to devote to his literary endeavors. In fact, Cthulhu was saddened to learn that this very issue will be the last *Tales of the Talisman*. Summers has decided that he wishes to spend more of his limited lifespan on his own writing, which Cthulhu understands goes in the more traditional chronological order. Mostly books about the Order of the Scarlet Steampunk Space Pirate Vampire Owls or some such thing. Tolerable if you enjoy that sort of thing. Most of what you spouted at me is dreck and nonsense. You think because you came up with an offbeat concept that the entire world should think it is as wonderful as you do and bow down and worship your brilliance. This is a fool's dream. Even as great, wonderful and insightful as the Dear Cthulhu columns are, not everyone enjoys them. People have different tastes. Those who like and enjoy dear Cthulhu have the good kind. The others have the wretched and bad variety.

    Writer's guidelines exist for a reason. Humans prefer for today to be similar to yesterday. When they watch or read something, most find it preferable to have some idea of what they are about to take in. For Summers or any other magazine editor to abruptly change what he or she has used to build an audience would likely spell the end of their publication, although admittedly in the case of *Tales of the Talisman* it really would not make much difference as this is the last issue.

    Perhaps you should take a look at your imagined and perceived literary talents and give them an honest assessment.

Hand off your work to others you trust and have high regard for. See what they think of your work. Join a writers group to get input from peers. Of course, another way is to simply keep sending out what you have written in hopes of finding an editor who feels the same way as you and is willing to publish and pay you for your work –good luck getting your requested advance without a scandal or popular reality show. Cthulhu has also heard the argument that people should just simply put their work up for sale and let the readers decide. This is an equally valid concept and easily done with the online venues available today. If after putting your work up for sale, you find that tens of thousands are paying money for your writing, your belief in your work's quality will be validated by voting by way of currency exchange. If instead you sell five copies and four are returned, then the opposite will be proved.

Or you can simply start your own magazine, one without guidelines, but make sure you have open submissions. I guarantee you will change your views on guidelines before your first issue comes out.

Dear Cthulhu,

I read with interest the letter in your column from the woman who was in love with and physically intimate with a duck and was troubled by the unusual nature of his member. I find myself in a similar predicament, abet with a different animal.

My husband and I bought a petting zoo and animal sanctuary years ago. I love animals and it's worked out pretty good overall. There have been a few bumps in the road like the time I found my husband offering to sell alpaca meat on the internet or when he decided it would be cheaper to feed the occasional pot-bellied pig to our mountain lion. The straw that broke the camel's back (not literally – thankfully our camels' spines are fine) was when my husband offered to send me off to a spa for three days and take care of all the animals while I was gone. Normally I do the mountain lion's share of the work. The zoo makes just enough money to pay our bills and keep going, so I hadn't been on a real vacation in years. I was a bit suspicious since he hadn't done anything that nice for me since we were courting, but really wanted the massage and seaweed wrap treatment, so I went. It took me hours and when I got there I was told nothing was paid for. I hadn't brought my credit cards so I turned around and went home. By the time I pulled into the driveway, it was dark and I was furious. The parking lot had cars I didn't recognize and there were lights on in the habitats. I snuck in and found out my husband was making some dirty deals. He had a couple of mobsters with a dead body they were trying to get rid of over by the pig pens and a bunch of guys in camouflage with guns who had paid him a grand each to hunt exotic animals. A flamingo may be exotic, but it's not exactly hard to shoot in a fenced enclosure.

Hubby was shocked to see me and even more surprised when I started throwing the hunters out. They wanted their money back and didn't want to leave until I pointed to our security cameras and asked to see their flamingo hunting licenses. I told them my husband and I were separated – as far as I was concerned it was only a matter of minutes until it happened – and to take it up with him.

Next, I turned toward the guys in suits who I thought were more hunters until I saw the corpse. Turns out Hubby owed ten grand for betting on cock fights, something he knows I hate for the unnecessary cruelty. He made a deal to help them get rid of dead bodies by feeding them to our pigs.

As soon as I saw the body, I hit the panic button on the alarm keychain I carried. It sent a signal to the zoo's security system.

I ran away and the mobsters chased me. I ducked into the nearest habitat which housed our kangaroo. Kenny had been declawed and mistreated by his previous owners and we had taken him in as a rescue. The mobsters followed me in and pointed guns at me. I've never been so scared in my life. I thought I was going to die. Then Kenny hopped out and boxed one man in the face and kicked the other man in the groin. Both hit the ground in pain.

By the time they got up, the cops had arrived. Luckily they hadn't been far. The cops have a speed trap where they hide behind one of our billboards about a mile down the road.

The cops captured the bad guys and with the dead body had enough to put them away. Hubby got convicted as an accessary after the fact and I got a quickie divorce. In exchange for me not testifying against him, he signed his half of the zoo over to me. The idiot didn't realize I'd already turned the security footage over, so the DA didn't need me to do anything to get a conviction. Especially since it showed him holding the gates open as the killers carried the body in for disposal.

I was happy to be rid of the deadbeat. I was even happier when I found out one of the crooks had a two hundred grand reward for their capture and because I'd summoned the cops, I got it.

You'd think my life would have been great, but it wasn't. I

was lonely. My ex was a loser, but he was good for one thing and it wasn't conversation.

Taking care of the animals was satisfying, but didn't take care of my womanly needs. I started having a glass of wine with dinner, then a bottle. One night I was drunk and wandering the paths and I came to Kenny's cage. I went inside and drunkenly told him thank you, then how lonely I was. He came up to me and I hugged him. Then I noticed the kangaroo was dry humping me. He was almost as tall as my short ex and only a little less hairy. I closed my eyes and it almost felt let I was holding a man who was thrusting against me. Maybe it was the loneliness or the white zinfandel, but some part of me decided it was a good idea to drop my jeans and let Kenny have his way with me. Part of it may have also been guilt that he was one of the few animals we hadn't been able to find a mate for and I knew that even a kangaroo guy had needs too.

I was so happy I did. OMG, it was amazing. The speed at which he took me was incredible, using those powerful legs to hump me like a freight train piston. And he felt bigger than my ex.

I had more orgasms than I ever had with a man.

It was only after the afterglow faded that I freaked out because I thought Kenny had two penises. Or is that peni? I looked closer and realized there were two ends.

I'm worried. Do you think Kenny has a conjoined twin that is attached to his penis? I checked but didn't see any teeth or eyeballs or other stuff. Does he need to have it removed? I hope not because the added width makes our special time together *really* amazing. Still, I'd hate for him to get hurt.

– Girl Down Under a Kangaroo

Dear Down Under,

There is nothing wrong with Kenny. Marsupials have a bifurcated penis. All kangaroos except the largest two species have this procreative feature. It helps them match up to the females which have two lateral vaginas. They can even store a fertilized embryo in the second of the corresponding wombs while another develops in the first and bring it to term later.

Your kangaroo is fine. However, you might want to check and make sure your procreative activities have not been caught by the cameras of your security system. While persecution for bestiality may not be a priority of your local District Attorney, it would not take long for video of your trans-species trysts to end up on the Internet if it fell into the wrong hands. And I cannot imagine that kind of publicity being good for what I assume would be considered a family friendly business. Use your reward money to build a private area in the kangaroo's habitat where you can enjoy each other away from prying eyes and cameras.

Dear Cthulhu,

I have a problem that I'm afraid it's going to ruin my life. I just landed a huge pharmaceutical rep job and my starting salary is more than both my parents make in a year. It's funny that I put it that way because my parents are at the root of my problem.

You see I'm terrified to drive.

It all goes back to when I was sixteen years old and I had just gotten my driver's permit. My dad had promised to take me for my driver's test. I couldn't find him or mom anywhere in the house, so I figured they must've gone out for a walk. They did that a lot. I always thought it was weird that with all the walking they did that they were still overweight. They should've been much skinnier.

I decided to wait in the car and went out to the garage. I got in the driver's seat and that's when the horror began.

I heard my mother and father groaning and screaming as if they were pain and I heard pounding like they were being beaten senseless. That's when I flipped the rearview mirror down and saw the most terrifying sight ever – my naked parents going at it in the back seat of the car, using positions I'd never even seen on the Internet. I tried to turn away, wanting to climb out of the car and run into the kitchen to wash my eyes out with bleach, but I couldn't move. I was stuck, frozen like a deer in headlights. They didn't even seem to realize or care that I was there. Finally, I slammed on the horn and that seemed to get their attention.

My father reminded my mother he had promised to take me for my driving test, so they had to finish up quickly. They started moving faster and screaming louder. From the buzzing, I think there might have been some sort of machinery involved. Eventually, they screamed so loud my ears rang for twenty minutes afterwards. When they disengaged, my naked mom leaned over the seat and kissed me on the cheek with the same mouth that moments earlier had been places I don't even want to mention and she wished me good luck.

My father told me to drive as he stayed in the back seat and put his clothes back on. I'm not sure how I made it to the driving test area. When dad got out, he was wearing his shirt and his pants inside out. I was mortified, but fortunately still in a state of shock. The driving instructor got in the car, told me what to do and I did it, completely on autopilot. Somehow, I still managed to get a perfect score and I got my driver's license. I've kept it up to date ever since.

Later that night I had to be hospitalized for an anxiety attack. I was so traumatized I worked ridiculously hard to graduate high school a year early just so I could go away to college sooner.

I still have nightmares, but thanks to the medication it happens only rarely. As a matter of fact, the medication is how I got offered this job. I became friends with a rep because I was trying to get the best medication to make more forget that horrible day. Eventually, I got an offer for an interview and then the job.

The problem is I have to drive over a several hundred-mile area to visit all the clients. I have not driven since the day of my driver's test. I can't. Every time I get in the driver's seat of a car, I get the shakes and break out in a cold sweat as soon as I realize there's a back seat.

After college, I didn't have any money so I've been working in a supermarket in walking distance of my parents' house, which I had to move back into because of the lack of funds. I need this job so I can get out of my parents' house and into a place of my own, far, far away.

Help me Cthulhu.

– Daunted Driver in Dubuque

Dear Daunted,

Although traumatic, it appears you've taken what happened to you and given it far too much importance. Procreation is a natural biological imperative. Your parents have a more than healthy procreation drive and the desire for each other. From writing my column, I can tell you that this is not always the case and, in all likelihood, contributes heavily to your parents staying together. It sounds like they were even courteous enough to leave the home proper before procreating up until that one time in the car.

Many advice-givers would recommend years and years of counseling while others would tell you just to put on your big boy jockeys and get over it. They are fools, overlooking the simple solution. And let's be honest - if it's not simple, most humans won't bother to do it.

You need to simply purchase a vehicle which has no backseat. A motorcycle would certainly qualify, but then you would have difficulty during winter and rainy times. There is a better solution. You are a young man and no one would think twice about you buying yourself a sports car. There are several brands to choose from which only have a front seat. That is right - no backseat to worry about or trigger your panic attacks. This should do you for a number of years, at least until there comes a time where you may decide to get a family of you own which will require a backseat for the children.

Cthulhu Happens

Dear Cthulhu,

I don't know if you're familiar with the new app Pokey-A-Guy Go, but it's all the rage. You take your phone and it uses the GPS to capture these mythical creatures on your phone in order to play a game. This game has changed my life and I don't even use it. Unfortunately, the program has put one of the rarest Pokey-A-Guy creatures in the middle of my living room. Ever since this got out, I've been having people breaking into my house day and night in order to get this Pokey-A-Guy. I've called the company and they had been less than responsive to my requests to change it. It's running into serious money. I've had to replace my window broken windows seven times and have even had to get the locks and even the door when it got knocked in on the door fixed.

The police are getting tired of responding to the break-ins. It's driving me nuts. What can I do?

– Pokey-A-Guy Pandemonium Sufferer in Poughkeepsie

Dear Sufferer,

The first thing you need to do is shore up your security and get better doors and lock. Then install video monitors and put up signs stating that you will prosecute. I know you said you did not have much money but my next bit of advice will help you to more than pay for it.

If these gamers are so fanatical that they'd be breaking into your home to get this virtual creature, then offer them the chance to come in and capture it for a hundred bucks cash each. This way you get a chance to control the traffic flow and take in some extra cash and these people get to play their game. It's a win-win for everyone.

Cthulhu Happens

Dear Cthulhu,

I read with interest your recent letter about the man whose girlfriend slept with the doll. My girlfriend does too, although it's a four-foot-tall beauty queen version of herself if she was impossibly proportioned.

"Barbara" typically has a doll sleeping on the opposite side of her from where I sleep. Barb had been ignoring my manly needs for a couple weeks, claiming the stress of work was too much and she wasn't in the mood. I woke up in the middle of the night rather excited and tried to put the moves on her. She shoved me away and said, "Here, bother mini-me instead." Then she handed me her doll before she rolled back over and went to sleep. Barb had left the doll laying on top of my excited part. I couldn't sleep and the doll was a miniature version of Barb, so I kind of had sex with it. It wasn't easy mind you because it doesn't have any holes, but I made do with the curves molded into the plastic.

As time went on, the pressures of Barb's job kept her pushing me away in the bedroom and I kept turning to Mini-Barb. And I was liking it.

Barb thought it was odd when I started buying clothes for her doll. She got even more confused when I started buying lingerie, but I got smart and bought the same outfits for both of them. That night Barb – the human one – actually joined me in the bedroom after putting the lingerie on her and her doll. For the first time in months, we made love together, but the whole time I was looking at the doll.

I think maybe Mini–Barb and I are a better match. The doll never nags me, never point out my flaws, and never turns me away when I'm in need sexually or tell me to stop because I'm being too freaky.

I think I'm more in love with the doll than I am with the woman. I'd like to break up with Barb, but I want to take the doll with me. Could Barb charge me with theft or kidnapping?

-Doll Man in Detroit

Dear Detroit,

As Cthulhu often points out, I am not a lawyer. There are some seas too dark for even Cthulhu to swim in. However, I am fairly certain that in order for kidnapping charges be brought, an actual living person has to be involved and a doll, no matter how lifelike, would not qualify.

Your soon to be former mate, however, could have you charged with theft. The severity of these charges could vary depending on how valuable the doll is. If there was a low monetary value, the charge would be a misdemeanor, but if it is some sort of collector's item that was valuable it could be a felony. If you are convicted of a felony, it could affect your ability to get and hold a job or even vote. Not that the people whom Cthulhu allows to run your country really give you much of a choice in that regard. There is a possibility that you would pay a fine or serve time. And the doll would then be returned to its original owner, separating you from the object of your twisted fixation.

You did not seem to think of the most obvious solution. Go on U-Bay and buy yourself a similar doll. This way your ex will not have any blackmail material to hold over your head if she figures out why you want the doll. If you find that you have an unusual fixation or emotional obsession with that particular hunk of plastic, then simply purchase the exact model and swap it out for the original when the woman is not home. Do this before you break up with her or breaking and entering or a burglary charges could also be added to the charges brought against you.

Dear Cthulhu,

I retired about ten years ago and was able to make ends meet until two years ago when my wife of forty-eight years passed away. It was devastating to lose my life partner. At least she went quickly. We were celebrating her seventy-seventh birthday by bungee jumping off a cliff and it was the attendant's first day on the job and he forgot to tie off the end of the bungee cord. At least she died happy – it was so quick I don't think she even realized the bungee cord snapped. Due to her cataracts, I don't even think she realized the ground was so close until after it snapped her neck.

As terrible it was as it was learning to live without the love of my life, things became even worse when I realized that I couldn't pay my bills without her pension. My wife and I have three adult children and I asked each of them if they would let me move in with them. Each of them has a guestroom and I even offered to help chip in towards household expenses.

All three of the ungrateful brats that I helped bring into this world, raised to adulthood, and put through college turned me down flat. They all had excuses – the grandkids were set into a certain pattern and they didn't want to disrupt it, their co-op board didn't allow guests to stay more than five days, that my playing the bagpipes at two in the morning would disturb the neighbors.

I was left with no choice but to sell my house and move into a nursing home. I hate it here. It doesn't feel like home. I'm required to tell someone if I go out. I have to spend time with a bunch of people who actually buy into the fact that they're old when they could be going out and doing the things they want to. They don't even have a gym or Zumba classes.

Then to top it all off my kids barely even visit me. They may show up on Christmas, Thanksgiving, Father's Day, and my birthday if I'm lucky. When they do show up, they've yet to hit the two-hour mark for a visit and never even offer to take me out to dinner or a movie or to parkour classes. It got to the point where last Thanksgiving I decided to mess with my selfish offspring. There are few people in the nursing home here who have Alzheimer's or dementia. Most of them are nice, but they can get rather annoying because they can have the same conversation with you, again and again, every fifteen minutes. When my kids showed up, I pretended like I had Alzheimer's and acted like I didn't recognize them. I'd seen enough from the folks in the home here that I was able to fake it pretty good. One of my two sons got lucky and somehow managed to marry himself a hottie, despite his dull personality. She always acted like she was bored in the marriage and had flirted with me on and off over the years.

Of course, I would never have dreamed of cheating on my wife when were married, but even a widower has needs. When Hotstuff came around, I pretended that I thought she was my late wife who I had always greeted with a kiss. It was never any of this peck on the lips nonsense. I swept my Loraine up into my arms, dipped her down, and kissed her passionately every time we reunited after being separated.

This time I called her Loraine and did the same to my daughter-in-law. At first, Hotstuff was shocked and started to push me away, but as I kissed her she realized she liked it. I doubt my milksop of son never kissed her half as passionately. By the end of the smooch, she had her hands wrapped around the back of my head and was trying to find my tonsils with her tongue. At this point my wimp of a son started hitting me on the back with a box of chocolate he brought me, yelling at me to let go of his wife. I turned around and shoved him away. Still in character, I told him no man was going to tell me that I couldn't kiss or make love to my wife. The grandkids, all teenagers, get some giggles out of it and Hotstuff let the wimp move her away, but she couldn't walk straight or take her eyes off of me. Ten minutes later Wimpy had his family in tow and was out the door.

I thought that was it and that I'd had my fun until two days later on Saturday Hotstuff shows up in my room at seven in the morning. My daughter-in-law shut and locked the door behind her. I'd just gotten out of bed and turned around and legitimately was a little confused. Then Hotstuff she opens up her long coat and she's got lingerie on underneath. She whispered, "Abner, it's me, Lorraine."

I just grinned. My daughter-in-law was actually pretending to be my dead wife. It was wrong on more than a few levels, but I hadn't been with anyone that young and good-looking in decades so I took her into my arms again. I kissed Hotstuff even longer than I had the first time and made mad, sweaty love to her and rode her longer than that bronco in the rodeo on my sixty-eight birthday.

Now Hotstuff comes by three or four times a week to visit. I found out the only good thing about the nursing home is the doctors are willing to prescribe almost anything you ask, including the little blue pill.

When Christmas rolled around, all three of my ungrateful kids came to visit with cheap gifts, but they left their spouses at home. That was okay because my daughter-in-law had already requested I stuff her stocking on Christmas Eve. She even made me dress up like Santa Claus. I shifted my acting into overdrive and started talking about my wife and I had an account in the Caymans and how was I going to get the money out and buy myself a new house. I may have insinuated that there were five hundred big ones there. They assumed it was half a million bucks. Many years ago on a cruise, Lorraine and I had set up an account in the Caymans on a lark and put a hundred dollars in it. With compound interest, it's now worth about five hundred bucks. So when my kids looked into it, the bank verified there was an account, but without the password wouldn't give out any more details.

Between Christmas and New Year's each of them visited me again but separately. They brought some decent gifts this time, trying to get the password for themselves. It didn't work and I wouldn't talk.

The wimp came up with the bright idea of having Hotstuff spend more time with me, pretending to be my wife – his mother. The milksop was willing to pimp out his wife in hopes that I'd give up the password to her so they could clean out my Cayman account. To her credit, Hotstuff only asked once and then used the extra time to get down to business.

Sometime in January, the brats petitioned a psychiatrist to determine my competency, claiming I was no longer fit to be in charge of my own finances. Since I'd never acted demented in front of any of the staff, the whelps were unable to get collaboration from anyone the nursing home. When I met with the shrink, I was my normal, charming self. He claimed that I did better on the cognitive tests than the average thirty-year-old. I got another prescription for the little blue pills and laid the groundwork for the folks at the nursing home to think that my children were wrongly trying to have me deemed incompetent so they could get control of my finances. Now, the greedy whippersnappers have to make an appointment to come see me, although my daughter-in-law is exempt and still visits frequently. I've even taken her out for dinner and dancing at one of these old time big-band clubs that the hipsters like. We go to concerts, movies, nightclubs, and I show Hotstuff a good time and she tells Wimpy that she's still impersonating my wife angle so as to get the password.

The reason why I am writing you is I've come I run out of ideas on how to torment my children for not taking me in when I needed them most. To be honest, my affair with my daughter-in-law has taken a lot of the edge off my anger and makes sure I get an aerobic workout several times a week. I seriously don't know how she does it. Without the blue pills, I'd have tapped out a while ago.

I need new ideas on how to mess with their heads without actually doing them any physical harm. I know from being a long-time reader of your column that this is right up your alley, so what do you have for me?

-Philandering Father in Fredericksburg

Dear Philandering,

Cthulhu cannot tell you how nice it is to receive a request from a human who actually has matters well in hand, but is just looking for a few pointers to up his game. It is a far cry from the letters I get from most of the rabble. Cthulhu is happy to help.

Pose with a big check like you won the Producers' Clearing House sweepstakes that has a million dollars printed on it. Make sure your money grubbing offspring see it and when they ask what happened to the money say you donated half to the Feed the Whales charity and used the other half to buy the Brooklyn Bridge.

Find a Photoshop expert or someone with a green screen. Prose for a few pictures and then don't communicate with your offspring for a week. Then have pictures printed up showing you in Paris, Tokyo, or Hawaii. They will think you went away and the fact that you are spending the non-existent money that they can't get ahold of will make them crazy.

Announce that you will leave your Cayman account to the person who can beat you in a battle of the bagpipes. Their learning and practicing will drive their families and neighbors crazy.

Tell them you had bought a very valuable coin collection recently and that you buried and would like to find. Make up a bizarre and twisted treasure map, tear it into pieces and leave enough clues for them to find the next piece of the map. You can have them running around town for weeks digging things up. When they finally find it, have it be a box of Murry Mozzarella tokens for them to find. When they ask you, play the dementia card again, saying you bought them for the grandkids.

Have fun tormenting your offspring.

If you have questions that Cthulhu can answer, and Cthulhu can answer all questions, please feel free to write. Sending sacrificial or financial offerings along with your questions is not necessary but is appreciated.

Have A Dark Day.

PATRICK THOMAS is the award-winning author of almost 40 books including the beloved fantasy humor Murphy's Lore series, which includes *Tales From Bulfinche's Pub, Fools' Day, Through The Drinking Glass, Shadow Of The Wolf, Redemption Road, Bartender Of The Gods, Nightcaps, Empty Graves, The Mug Life* — as well as the future space adventures *Startenders* and *Constellation Prize*.

The Murphy's Lore After Hours spin-offs star the half pixie/ogre Terrorbelle (*Fairy With A Gun, Fairy Rides The Lightning* and *Terrorbelle The Unconquered*); the former demon-possessed serial killer Agent Karver of the Department of Mystic Affairs (*Dead To Rites, Rites of Passage*); the cursed magi Hex (*By Darkness Cursed and By Invocation Only*); Vince Argus, the Soul For Hire (*Greatest Hits*); and Negral, a forgotten Sumerian god who works as Hell's Detective (*Lore & Dysorder* and *Bullets & Brimstone*).

Co-Written with John French and Diane Raetz, his Mystic Investigators paranormal mystery series includes *Mean Streets* and the omnibus editions *Shadows & Bullets & Brimstone* and *Once Upon In Crime*. *Assassin's Ball*, his first mystery, is also co-written with John French.

His works include the steampunk *As The Gears Turn* and the space epic *Exile & Entrance*. He co-edited *New Blood* and *Hear Them Roar* and was an editor for the magazines *Fantastic Stories of the Imagination* and *Pirate Writings*.

Patrick's darkly humorous advice column Dear Cthulhu has been running since 2005 and includes the collections *Have A Dark Day, Good Advice For Bad People, Cthulhu Knows Best, Cthulhu Happens, Cthulhu Explains It All* and *What Would Cthulhu Do?* Dear Cthulhu appears monthy on the radio show *Destinies: The Voice of Science Fiction* which is hosted by Dr. Howard Margolin.

His short stories have been featured in over sixty anthologies and more than forty-five print magazines.

A number of his books were part of the props department of the CSI television show and Nightcaps was even thrown at a suspect's head. His urban fantasy Fairy With A Gun had been optioned for film and TV by Laurence Fishburne's Cinema Gypsy Productions. Top Men Productions has turned his Soul For Hire Story, *Act of Contrition*, into a short film.

Please drop by www.patthomas.net or follow him at I_PatrickThomas at Twitter or www.facebook.com/PatrickThomasAuthor to learn more.

Help is only a Rainbow Away...

"Mix Gaiman's American Gods and Robinson's Callahan's Crosstime Saloon on Prachett's Discworld and you get an idea of Thomas' Murphy's Lore." -David Sherman, author of STARFIST and Demontech

"ENTERTAINING, INVENTIVE AND DELIGHTFULLY CREEPY." -JONATHAN MABERRY, New York Times and Bram Stoker Award Winning Author

"SLICK... ENTERTAINING." -Paul Di Filippo, ASIMOV'S

"HUMOR, OUTRAGEOUS ADVENTURES, & SOME CLEVER PLOT TWISTS." -Don D'Ammassa, SCIENCE FICTION CHRONICLE

PATRICK THOMAS

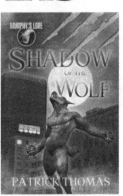

One Last Chance to Save
Happily Ever After

Can a group of heroes including Goldenhair, Red Riding Hood and Rapunzel help General Snow White and her dwarven resistance fighters defeat the tyrannical Queen Cinderella? And will they succeed before a war with Wonderland destroys everything?

Their only hope to stop Cinderella's quest for power lies with a young girl named Patience Muffet who carries the fabled shards of Cinderella's glass slippers.

Roy Mauritsen's fantasy adventure fairy tale epic begins with *Shards Of The Glass Slipper: Queen Cinder*.

"Fantastic...
A Magnificent Epic!"
-Sarah Beth Durst, author of
Into The Wild & *Drink, Slay, Love*

"The Brothers Grimm
meets
Lord Of The Rings!"
-Patrick Thomas, author
of the Murphy's Lore series

"Shards is a dark, lush, full-throttle fantasy epic that presents a bold re-imagining of classic characters."
-David Wade, creator of
319 Dark Street

"Roy Mauritsen's enchanting epic comes at a time when fairy tales are back in the forefront of our collective imagination."
-Darin Kennedy,
short fiction author

PADWOLF
PUBLISHING

In paperback & e-book
Find out more at:
shardsoftheglassslipper.com
padwolf.com

IT'S A CRIME TO MISS THESE GREAT STORIES!

from author
John L. French

WWW.PADWOLF.COM

You can't get better than 13!

DOWN THESE MEANS STREETS
of Magic & Monsters walk the

MYSTIC INVESTIGATORS

CPSIA information can be obtained
at www.ICGtesting.com
Printed in the USA
BVHW040316060722
641299BV00010B/1411